Ch

Table of Contents

Acknowledgements............................2

Chapter One..4

Chapter Two......................................55

Chapter Three...................................90

Chapter Four..................................125

Chapter Five....................................174

Space Whale Dreams

Shannon Frances Smith

Champion of Seasons

ACKNOWLEDGMENTS

Written by Shannon Frances Smith

Edited by Angela Brown

Cover Art Illustrated by Ceylon Animations

Published through Space Whale Dreams

Copyright 2023 all rights reserved

Champion of Seasons

Champion of Seasons

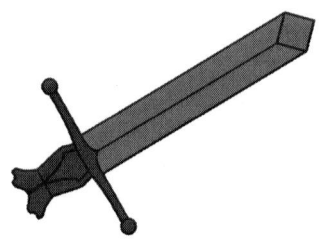

CHAPTER ONE

Ice clung to the walls of the cave as Lyn sat by the fire, burdened with memories she would rather bury. She looked over the packs she had recovered from her traveling companions. A tall woman in her mid-twenties with the tanned complexion of a working girl, green eyes, and blond hair tied in a messy braid, she wore a cotton cloak of many stitches, a haphazard mess

Champion of Seasons

of materials roughly tied together. Under that, a sweat-stained blouse and trousers made for travel.

She picked through the obscene pile of rations, sorting between dried fruit and various smoked meats. At the start of this journey, her travelling companions had argued over whether this would be enough food to feed everyone and debating buying more. Now it was only her; some of the dried and smoked food would go bad before she could possibly eat it.

Nevertheless she grabbed some bacon and dried dates bound in cloth and held them over the fire to defrost them. Mount Kikica was frigid after all; everything here seemed to freeze. Quietly, slowly, she ate the food without tasting or taking any joy in it. She tossed the wrappings into the fire and watched them burn.

She lay down next to the fire with her bedroll, a second one on the ground below it for extra comfort. It wasn't like the person who owned it before was going to use it anytime soon. She let her tears fall and be evaporated by the heat of the fire, her thoughts never leaving the remnants of the fight.

The journey Lyn and her group had started was over, and the destination hadn't been reached. Looking into the embers, she knew in her heart this was the end. Her companions, people she had known from a village that seemed an eternity away, people who had been dear to her, and some she had grown up with— all gone in a few moments.

Champion of Seasons

Finally Lyn stopped crying and drifted off to sleep. Her dreams were nightmarish visions of large wooly monsters baring teeth and claw, ice and snow falling like daggers being thrown by trained assassins—and the gore...by the *gods,* the gore. Sleep was fitful, and she found herself fighting it. She knew, somehow, the visions of terror could see her. She also knew she should have shared the others' fate, yet somehow she'd survived.

Eventually she gave up on sleep, sitting up and staring into the fire. Only the wind whistled through the cavern. In that still moment, Lyn bowed to the flames then chanted:

"Oh, God up high, I have seen what no one should see, and I wish not to live

Champion of Seasons

with this in my memory. I do not want to be among the living. This mountain shall become my grave, for I should die with my companions, who shall never feel the warm glow of the sun or the green meadows of our home. Why should I? Fate could not have a plan for me if it didn't have a plan for them."

    She sat by the fire as the light flicked and danced. After an unmeasurable time, the crackle of the fire was joined by the soft sobs of a young woman…no, not her —someone else. The sound echoing from the darkness of the cave grabbing her attention, she looked in its rough direction and called out, "Is someone there?"

    An answer came out from the shadows deep within the cave: "Help. Please help. I want to see my mother."

Champion of Seasons

The voice came from a petite woman who appeared to be in her late teens, lying in the fetal position. She had auburn hair—a red that almost glowed—laced with white flowers. Her eyes were a bright, almost-sapphire blue. Her complexion was creamy, and she was dressed like nobility, wearing a brown fur coat and a pink frock dress.

"We were ambushed," the girl said. "I survived, but the guards I was with... Oh, by the gods... Please, miss, can you help me? I need to get to Mother's! She would worry something dreadful if I don't arrive home."

"You're passing through this mountain at this time of the year?" Lyn looked at the girl skeptically.

"Aren't you as well?" the girl replied, catching her breath between sobs.

"Fair point," Lyn said as she looked at her supplies from the journey past. "I will help you," she finally said after a long pause, her good nature getting the better of her. "Do you have a name?"

"I'm…Kora," the girl replied. "And you?"

"Lyn. Where is your mother's home?"

"I can show you!" Kora smiled as she stood up, her frock swaying under her coat. "Thank you so much!" She wiped the tears from her eyes.

Lyn sighed. "Can't you at least tell me where she is?"

Champion of Seasons

"Well..." Kora looked to her feet. "I don't think you'd believe me if I told you."

"And you can't just walk on your own because—"

"Look at me! You think I can defend myself?"

Lyn couldn't argue with the fact that she was indeed looking at a woman who was younger than her and acted accordingly. Poor girl might as well be wearing a ROB ME! sign on her back. After another long pause, Lyn said, "Okay...but you'd better know where you're going."

"Oh, you can trust me!" Kora said with a look of relief. "I've taken this trip for some time now, every year, without fail."

"How far is it?"

Champion of Seasons

"Not too far, I promise!"

"Just let me grab the supplies. Then we can get out of here."

After Lyn gathered what she could into her pack, the two headed outside. Kora calmed down during that moment. As they saw the light of the sun through the cave entrance, Lyn felt something wash over her, a strange warmth that was almost energizing but soothing too.

"That should help you feel less weary, Lyn," Kora said with a confident smile.

"Thank you..." Lyn's voice trailed off. "Are you some sort of magick user?"

"Uh...you can say that, sure. I just want to help—it's within our best interests, both of ours, to make it down the mountain safely."

Champion of Seasons

Lyn looked back to the cave entrance with a sombre glare in her eyes, remembering her prayer to the High God. "Let's get going."

Kora caught that look in Lyn's eyes. "You would want to stay here?" she intuitively asked. "It's cold and desolate, and...well...cold."

"It's...complicated, Kora," Lyn replied sadly. "I lost my travelling companions, and I would... Well...I really would rather... But you need someone to be with you going down the mountain."

Kora went deep in thought, then filled in the blanks Lyn had left in her words and came to a horrifying conclusion. "So you want to be dead with them? That seems silly! Just be happy you're alive at this moment!"

"If only I could. It doesn't feel right; I don't expect you to understand," Lyn replied.

As the two walked, Kora pointed to a path. "This way."

Lyn looked at the path and recoiled, for she recognized it right away. "Must we?"

"Well, otherwise it would be a journey of several nights, in this weather. This way we'll be at the base of the mountain by nightfall."

Lyn let out a sigh and looked back at Kora. "Fine."

They didn't walk far before Kora saw why Lyn didn't want to come out here. In a mound barely covered in snow were frozen corpses, mangled and gnawed on, lying in crumpled positions. There were five in all. Lyn winced and took two steps back.

"Charming," Kora said. "I've seen better welcoming parties than this."

"Welcoming party!" Lyn burst out sourly. "You brat, those are... They're... I was on a pilgrimage, and they..."

"Easy." Kora placed a hand on Lyn's shoulder. "Didn't realize they were once your people. They look like they've been dead for three, maybe four days. Were you in that cold cave that long?"

Lyn nodded. "I should be with them," she muttered. "It feels wrong that I am alive and they're..." She trailed off.

"Can you introduce me?" Kora asked with a faint smile.

Lyn glared at her. "What?"

Champion of Seasons

"They must have been important to you for you to be this worked up about their..." Kora took a graver tone. "Who were they? I really want to know."

Lyn walked towards the bodies, one by one. First she pointed to an older man in once-bright white vestments now stained by blood and dirt. His neck was bent at an unnatural angle, his head barely hanging on to the shoulders, his back twisted. "That's Father Triff. He led our pilgrimage," Lyn began. "He was a good man, a pillar of the community."

"Oh." Kora had a curious look in her eyes "A pilgrimage?! Where were you going? Where are you from?"

"Mabe, in the southern region," Lyn replied. "We were going to the temple of the High God."

Champion of Seasons

"Oh, that grand place!" Kora smiled. "Please tell me more about Father Triff."

"He was a kind-hearted man but also very strict about piety," Lyn remarked. "Always made us pray the rosary, and we got a good scolding for messing up a line in the Creed of the High God's Disciple."

"So, like most priests I've met," Kora replied.

Lyn gave the girl a sore look.

"Sorry," Kora said. "Please continue."

"And that's Ella." Lyn pointed to a girl no older than sixteen with braided black hair and wearing a worn, ripped cloak. "She and I were training to be nuns for the High God. In a way, I envied her for her body, which was pure and unbroken. She would have had an easier time getting in."

"Pure? And you're not?" Kora remarked with surprise. "You seem pure of heart to me."

"Ella had never been sullied by a man, I mean," Lyn replied. "I...I had a relationship with a boy back in my village. Such a stupid decision."

"Oh, you mean virginity!" Kora loudly concluded. "Between you and me, it's overrated."

"Sure." Lyn continued with her reminiscence. "Ella was a shy girl, especially around men, so she clung to Paige and me a lot." She pointed to an older woman with greying hair and wearing earth tones. "Paige, our den mother, was always taking care of us,

Champion of Seasons

making sure we were eating and getting up at the right times and praying every day—much like a mother would. She really saw us as her charges.

"And of course, Jason, that rascal." Lyn gestured to a brown-haired teenage boy in a knitted coat. "His parents made him go on this pilgrimage to have discipline forced into him. He complained the entire way when he wasn't placing buckets on top of doorways, stringing up everyone's underwear, or running off with Father Triff's hat... He was a wild card, that one."

"So he was a rascal with pushover parents," Kora uttered.

Lyn paused. She turned to look at Kora, then back at Jason's body. "Basically," she agreed, knowing that as insulting as that was, it was true. "I mean, if I did half the stuff he did, my bottom would have been bright red! 'Course, he was sent to redeem himself. Never had the chance."

"He looks different." Kora pointed to the last of the dead pilgrims—this one was in mail armour that had splintered rings along the chest.

"That was Del," Lyn stated. "He was along for the ride more than anything else. We pooled some money to hire him as muscle against bandits and wild animals. We didn't know much about him. He seemed brave and wasn't particularly religious.

"He was the first to fall." Lyn looked away from the bodies as a tear escaped her eye and froze to her face. "We were

Champion of Seasons

walking through here, and a yeti ambushed us. The monster was fast and strong. Del screamed at us to run ahead while he swung at it, but the thing killed him so quickly.

"The rest of us ran, but..." Lyn pointed to a cliff above them. "It avalanched. I was the only one who wasn't caught. And then the yeti attacked. I fled into the cave, and that's where I've been since."

"You blame yourself for their deaths?"

"In a way I should have joined them," Lyn meekly conceded. "I mean, how did the snow miss me?"

"It missed you because it did." Kora shrugged. "I don't understand why this is a point of contention for you."

Champion of Seasons

"What do you mean?!" Lyn sneered at the girl. "My companions and I came together; we were pilgrims before the High God. I'm nothing special—if the Fates don't have a plan for them, why should they have a plan for me?"

"Well, because they do?" Kora shrugged again. "Whatever plan they have, they decided you need to live. No one said the Fates are nice about it."

Lyn looked at the bodies of Ella and Jason. "Those two were too young to die." She then pointed to Paige and Father Triff. "And they were guiding us and could have guided more people. Del? He died serving his sworn duty. Had he lived, he could have saved many more lives."

"Lyn, it's sad, I know," Kora replied solemnly while placing a hand on her new

Champion of Seasons

friend's shoulder. "But the Fates don't concern themselves with these things, and there's nothing we can do about it now. Just be happy you're alive...for you, like any of us, can die at any time. Now this way. We need to get down the mountain..."

Kora's words died in her throat as loud footsteps echoed from the path. The two looked up to see a gigantic furry monster standing over them, a look of hunger and rage in its red eyes and bloodstains on its white fur. It stood over ten feet tall, towering over them. A yeti...the yeti that most likely had killed Lyn's companions. Lyn and Kora watched the snow slide down and cover the way back.

Champion of Seasons

Lyn ran up to Del's body and pried his sword from his frozen hands. She almost fell from the blade's weight—a blade she witnessed the muscular man wield effortlessly with one hand. She, however, could barely carry the thing with two. With the adrenaline pumping through her veins, the weapon was quickly in her hands, and she swung it wildly at the beast. "No, no, no," she called. "You will not!"

The yeti paused to look at them, eyes curious and licking its lips. Its red eyes stared down at Lyn as she held up the shiny weapon under the cold sun. The beast charged, the weight of its raging body making the ground rumble.

"That's it, Lyn. Distract the thing," Kora whispered as Lyn faced the snow

Champion of Seasons

beast, which snarled with animalistic hunger. Fear of this thing gave way to fury within Lyn as she struggled with the cold metal of the heavy weapon.

As the beast charged, Lyn clumsily swung the blade, hitting its thigh with the broad side of the weapon. The beast bellowed in pain as it swung its paw at Lyn, knocking her to the ground, the sword crashing with a clatter. She rolled to get out of the way of the yeti as it attempted to pounce on her, the ground shaking even more as she reached for the sword. Screaming, she swung it up from the ground and towards the yeti. She slashed its chest as the momentum of the blade made her roll around on the ground. She then struggled to her feet, shaking from pain as she grunted to herself from the weight of Del's sword.

The yeti made a grab for her. Lyn's attempt to jerk out of the way was in vain as its claws wrapped around her waist and lifted. Wildly she swung the sword at the yeti in a desperate attempt to get the beast off her. The creature howled as the tip of the blade caught its mouth and it recoiled. This was long enough for Lyn to get in another good swing, which made purchase with the beast's cheek. Roaring in agony, it dropped her to the ground.

The drop knocked the wind out of her as the blade fell, broadside parallel to the ground, on top of her. She cried out in pain as she struggled to her feet again, only for the yeti to be on her. Weakly she swung the weapon but missed making any connection to the yeti as the creature's hot, rotten breath was on her face—it was going to bite her.

Except Lyn's fight had given Kora enough time. Lyn was too busy to notice Kora as she held out her palms to the corpses. Her eyes went white as she made mana channel from her feet into the ground around them. As though she were calling out for something, she whispered, "How did my honey teach this? Do I remember what he taught me?"

Through sanguine channelling of mana, black ichor flowed from the ground by Kora's feet and into the five frozen corpses of Lyn's former companions, seeping into their frozen bodies. The corpses began to stir and lift themselves from the snow and ice.

Champion of Seasons

The sound of the moving bodies grabbed the yeti's attention, and it saw the horrifying sight. Five frozen zombies: Ella, Jason, Paige, Del, and Father Triff. All of them charging towards the yeti. They each grabbed the monster, which roared as it shook and flailed to shake off their cold, hard grips.

Lyn gawked in horror at the sight of the pilgrims' animated corpses grasping the yeti. She stumbled back onto her feet and grabbed for Del's sword without taking her eyes off the gross sight. In the frozen moment of the zombies holding down the yeti, she found an opening. She tightened her grip on Del's sword while writhing in pain from the yeti's previous attacks. Lyn got up and swung the sword, catching the yeti in the gut, and the thing

Champion of Seasons

toppled to the ground. Her arms shook as she pulled the blade out of the monster, its blood and entrails spilling onto her. Bracing itself, the yeti attempted to stand. Lyn knew she couldn't let the beast get back up again, and with a near-blind swing, the sword cut past the yeti's desperate attempt to block the weapon and slashed its jugular, sending it back to the ground.

As the yeti's blood pooled and became red ice on the cold mountain ground, the zombies collapsed in a heap on its fresh corpse. Lyn took a moment to catch her breath as Kora approached her. Green mana flowed from Kora and into Lyn, attempting to close the gaping wound on her shoulder.

Champion of Seasons

Lyn recoiled, the mana flashing away into the aether. "Wha...wh-who *are* you?" she stammered, scrambling away from her friends' corpses.

"I told you... I'm Kora. I just want to see my mother. That's all!"

"How...how..." Lyn paced between Kora and the mound of bodies. "Necromancy!"

"I'm sure seeing your friends like that was upsetting," Kora spoke with a grim expression. "But we need to survive to see my mother and for you to go home too—wherever home would be for you. Besides, the souls that entered those bodies were souls standing around in Acheron, bored out of their minds because they couldn't pay the fare to get into the Underworld—and a corpse is nothing but

Champion of Seasons

an empty shell. In a way, we entertained some ghosts in exchange for their help."

Lyn stopped pacing and looked into Kora's sapphire eyes. After a long pause, she said, "Please tell me your mother isn't some lich. You know, the kind we hear about in campfire stories who animate the dead and feast on their essence."

"My mother is the exact opposite of a lich queen," Kora said, sounding offended. "She's all about nature and plants, and I get to help with her gardens whenever I'm—"

"All right," Lyn muttered. "Let's keep going...but no more funny business."

"Nothing funny about this adventure, I will say that much!" Kora replied with a nervous grin, "Now let me finish with that wound. It's got to hurt, and you wouldn't want an infection."

Lyn let Kora finish healing her shoulder wound, the green mana flowing warmth and energy into her arm. She then approached the corpses and, with a wince, took the scabbard and baldric off Del, slung the baldric across her shoulder so it hung at her left hip, and sheathed her new sword. The two pressed onward. As they walked, the sun shone brightly and the snow began to melt. It was beginning to feel so warm Lyn opened her cloak as the two of them walked. As the day turned into night, and the base of the mountain was in sight, the two heard wolves howling in the distance.

"We can't camp here," Lyn whispered. "Wolves are on the prowl."

Champion of Seasons

The two continued to walk while keeping vigilant eyes out for the glowing orbs of any predators that could be lurking, ready to pounce on them. It was tiring to keep a steady march, but the alternative was a wolf attack, which Lyn didn't want to risk. Her eyes darted around every time she heard a howl. Kora walked behind her, her panting breath rasping through the darkness. There was nothing but the moon to light their way.

As the howling carried on throughout the night, Lyn was sure there were other beasts of prey in the dark that could easily take down a human being. Still, the two were silent as dawn broke. They'd reached the base of the mountain, where it turned into a snow-covered meadow...except Lyn noted the snow was dripping off the grass.

"By the High God, spring is almost upon us," Lyn remarked. "My companions and I were on that mountain for a long time."

"Odd decision to climb a mountain in the dead of winter."

"We debated it, and Father Triff decided the shortened travel time outweighed the risks the mountain posed to us." Lyn had a frustrated look in her eyes.

"So he got the group killed?" Kora asked. "I mean, this was his idea, and I hate to say it, but he should have taken the long way around...or better yet, not marched with a group of pilgrims in winter. Should have hunkered down and waited for the spring, at least."

"Well, we were told we had to go when we did or we'd miss the eclipse solstice. Being at the temple at that time would give extra blessings, which we all could have used to become nuns and be disciplined or whatever else," Lyn justified.

Kora gave a solemn nod. "Fate made its judgement. I'm sorry, Lyn."

Lyn deeply thought on this. At the time her group had planned their journey, the mountain had appeared to be a death trap. She remembered saying as much at the time, but Father Triff had reassured them the High God would see them through.

Champion of Seasons

"You're right, Kora. Father Triff was a reckless fool—but we believed he knew best," Lyn replied.

"Being a man of the High God and all?" Kora smirked. There was a quiet pause. She then continued more seriously: "This absolves you. They didn't need to die, and you didn't need to be dead with them."

Sighing, Lyn stared into the distance. Maybe it absolved her, but she couldn't shake the memory of watching them die or how she was able to avoid their fate.

The two took a nap on the soft grass and ate some aged bacon and withered dates Lyn had on her. Soon they were on the move again, with Kora leading the way. They marched along a path in a

Champion of Seasons

wooded area when a voice called out, "Hey, ladies!"

The two turned to see a man with black hair and brown eyes. He wore a bandana on his face and ragged leather armour.

"Can we help you, kind sir?" Kora asked.

"Yeah, ya could," he replied. "Ya can just throw yer coin purse to me."

"Oh...excuse me?" Kora dumbly asked.

"Ya deaf, pumpkin? I said the two of y'all will leave yer coin purses with us."

"*Us?*" Kora grimaced. The two looked to see another similar-looking man behind them, and more on their two o'clock, four o'clock, seven o'clock, and ten o'clock as well, stalking the woods.

Champion of Seasons

"Leave us be!" Lyn barked. "We have nothing of value."

"Ya kidding?" the leader scoffed. "Nutten?" He reached for a dagger in his belt. "That ain't true t'all, ladies. We haven't had fun in a long time. Right, boys?" The others each had a weapon drawn: one had a bow and arrow; one had a spiked club; and the rest held daggers. "With that in mind, strip!" he commanded.

As he spoke, a wrestling in the nearby greenery ensued. Lyn looked around, as did the bandits, and saw a bright-green aura emanating from Kora, one that extended from her body and into the nearby trees and shrubs. The plant life quickly began to grow—the branches, vines, thorns, and stems moving in all directions around them. Looking confused, the men scrambled, but at the end of it, only one of them was able to avoid being caught up in the greenery.

"Wha...?" one of the bandits stammered as he saw his colleagues trapped. Readying his dagger, he said, "I don't know what foul magick ya have, but I gotta put an end to this!" He lunged at Kora, but Lyn had enough time to unsheathe her sword, and she swung it at the man, gutting him. She stood in shock as he collapsed and lay on the ground in a pool of blood.

"Oh, now ya've done it!" the leader growled from his tangle of branches. "Killing Goto is overkill. Right? Bitches!"

As he spoke, proving how foolish he and his crew truly were, the plants moved

Champion of Seasons

again, providing an opening for Lyn and Kora to run through. They did so, leaving the bandits to painstakingly fight their way out of the thicket Kora had created.

"Did I just..." Lyn stammered as they walked side by side through the woods.

"You only did what had to be done," Kora replied.

"Yeah, but—"

"But nothing! Those men would have killed us or worse if not for you. Thank you!" Kora responded with a faint smile.

"I mean, I'm not a killer... I don't want to kill..." Lyn continued in her minor panic. "I was... The way he... And the blood... All from my hand..."

Champion of Seasons

"You didn't have this issue with the yeti."

"The yeti wasn't human," Lyn replied. "That man...was."

"Lyn, I understand." Kora said with a faint smile. "However, you were defending yourself and me—his death was justified, and they were the ones stupid enough to tempt fate in the first place. They could—and should—be able to earn an honest living through hard work, but instead they were demanding people give them things by flexing their might. It's barbaric. Mother has explained to me how brutal nature can be, with lions eating antelope, and he tells me death is an inevitability."

"Who's 'he'?" Lyn asked, curious.

Champion of Seasons

The question went unanswered as, through the trees, a river could be seen. Its edges still had bits of ice, but the center had thawed and was flowing ever so fast.

"Not much farther," Kora pointed out. "We'll be boarding a boat here and going out into the water—not that far out, of course."

They walked along a pathway that led to the riverbank, where a small boat was hitched up. The boat, barely big enough for the two of them, featured a sail with a wheat sheaf design finely embroidered on it. The mahogany ship looked ready for the two to board.

Kora approached the boat and gestured for Lyn to follow.

"We aren't stealing a boat, are we?" Lyn asked uneasily.

Champion of Seasons

"Oh, no, no, we aren't. Mother left this here. It's a present from the king of seas."

"The king of seas?" Lyn said slowly.

"He's fun at parties, though he has a nasty temper," Kora explained. "He gave the boat to Mother to shorten the travel time for me!"

Lyn's eyes narrowed on Kora. "That better be the truth."

"Promise!" As they boarded, Kora looked to the water. "There's the water, flowing, down to a stream," she remarked, "flowing as time does, down the stream and over time, eroding the banks and carrying minerals into the sea. Changing the world around it yet remaining flowing like a river flows."

Champion of Seasons

"Right," Lyn replied slowly as she boarded the boat, grabbing a paddle to align it as Kora unhitched the vessel. "Time flows... I wish I didn't have to witness it anymore, what with my fellow pilgrims dead on a mountain. Like I said, I should have died with them..."

"But Lyn, you didn't die on the mountain," Kora cooed. "You're on this boat with me!"

Lyn sighed. "I...I only agreed to this because I felt bad for you. I would have stayed on that mountain otherwise."

"Why feel bad?" Kora smirked. "Why feel bad for poor little me?"

"I... You're an innocent in all this... and you needed someone to help you, as you insisted...and you shouldn't be dragged down into the dead mire I'm in—

Champion of Seasons

and should be in," Lyn answered as the ship sailed down the river with the momentum of the flowing water, breaking through the thinning ice along the way.

"Isn't the sun beautiful?" Kora asked, lifting her face towards it, feeling it radiate upon her skin.

"If I could look at it without going blind, I could tell you," Lyn responded, a faint smile on her lips.

"Hey! You're smiling!" Kora rejoiced as they broke through the remaining ice into open water. "Your face is lifting and everything! Wow, you're pretty when you smile!"

"Am I?" Lyn then returned to her sad grimace.

"And to think, if not for me, you would've never seen the sun like this

Champion of Seasons

again!" Kora replied with a playful smile and a side-glance.

Lyn got quiet, thinking. Kora was right: the sun on the mountain was usually blocked by cloud cover, and it would have felt cold in the elevated air. The two were quiet as the boat joined the river in emptying out into the sea and the wind caught the sail and blew it on course. Soon there was nothing but the deep blue sea in all directions.

"We just need to follow the wind and trust the gods of storm and sea," Kora stated. "Both of them have a vested interest in seeing me join Mother."

"The gods?" Lyn lifted one eyebrow sardonically. "Sure they do. I'm trusting we aren't on a wild goose chase in the middle of the ocean."

Champion of Seasons

"We're not, I promise."

Moments later, the sky went dark. Lyn looked to Kora, whose normally cheery demeanour had changed into a mix of anger and fear. "Oh, no," she growled. "It's the kraken!"

"What?" Lyn looked at Kora, confused. That's when the tentacles came out from the water in front of them and lashed out at the boat. "Th-that ..." Kora stammered.

In a panic, the two adjusted the sails to change course. More tentacles appeared from the water and made desperate grabs for them and the small boat. Kora knelt on the deck; a moment later, her green aura wrapped around the boat. "Damn it!" she said angrily. "This is the sea god's domain! I only have so much sway here."

Champion of Seasons

"You can raise the dead, but you can't do anything in the water?" Lyn shouted in confusion.

"I have no dominion over the sea. I can have the ship sprout plant growth, but what would that do? The sea god is very testy. I don't know why."

The kraken's head broke the surface of the water, its eyes trained on the boat as it used its tentacles to create a whirlpool in an attempt to pull the vessel closer. The motion made some of the water turn to mist and created the illusion of rain falling on them. The water quickly became very rough, with the two women desperately holding on to the mast.

As the boat helplessly drifted closer to the kraken, the creature's orange eyes with rectangular pupils stared at the boat

Champion of Seasons

while its massive tentacles reached for the women. It missed them but wrapped around the boat and began to pull it closer.

"No!" Kora screamed. "We were so close to our destination!"

Lyn got a desperate idea. As the enormous tentacle reached for them, she pulled out Del's sword and wrapped her legs around the mast to keep from falling from the weight of the weapon. She swung it at one tentacle, then the one that was around the boat. Blue blood mixed with the water and spilled into the vessel. Kora placed a hand on the boat's railing. As Lyn made another swing at the tentacle, she noticed the boat was growing thorns around the hull. The tentacles still kept coming, slower and bleeding but still pulling the boat closer to the kraken.

In the chaos, a tentacle wrapped around Lyn; she felt the slimy, sucking sensation of its puckers all over her flesh. She swung at the tentacles as they wrapped themselves around her and pulled the boat closer towards it. Lyn had a moment of clarity when she unwrapped her legs from the mast. Perhaps this was what fate meant for her: that she die so Kora could get home.

Lyn thrashed as she was pulled into the cold seawater, but she cut enough of the monster's flesh that she was able to free the sword from the tentacles. Still, the need to breathe made her panic as her lungs burned for air. Lyn pried and swung as much as she could, thrashing, swinging,

Champion of Seasons

and kicking violently, feeling the tentacles strangle her. Soon she was kicking at a hard part of the kraken—its beak.

Desperation took hold of her as she carved her way out of the soft tissue of the monster and kicked to the surface. She inhaled a gulp of air before more tentacles grabbed her and pulled her into the water again. Lyn this time had an idea: as the tentacles pulled her towards its maw again, she thrusted upwards with the blade. Lyn climbed the monster, using the heavy weapon to keep her from slipping and fighting the force of the water to cut the kraken. She made gash after gash, the beast lowering into the water, giving Lyn a target as she sank from the weight of the blade. She made one last strike, thrusting the heavy weapon between the kraken's eyes.

When the blade pierced one of the creature's eyes, it roared in pain as it sank into the depths of the sea, its tentacles going with it and the whirlpool subsiding. The sky became clear again, and the water stopped sloshing into the boat. Lyn swam up to the surface and towards the battered boat, which she then attempted to board.

"Lean on the boat that way," Lyn commanded Kora to keep the vessel from capsizing as Lyn boarded. Kora complied, which kept the boat steady enough to let Lyn aboard.

"Good thinking!" Kora exclaimed as she held out her palm.

Champion of Seasons

Lyn slapped it, then slumped onto the deck. "Hope I don't need that weapon anytime soon," she replied, exhausted.

"Once we're with my mother, we shouldn't need to be armed." Kora lay down next to Lyn. "She lives in a peaceful place."

The sail had a few rips in it, and the body of the boat was thorny, with the pain of those thorns now making themselves known on Lyn's battered body.

"Who is the king of seas?" she asked wearily.

"He's one of the three kings," Kora replied. "There's also the king of storms and the king of the dead."

"The old gods, it sounds like," Lyn breathed.

Champion of Seasons

"Each of the elder ones have their domains, the places they rule supreme over," Kora explained. "Then there are the queens—the queen of nature and the queen of hearth."

"Pagan. Great. That's exactly what I need," Lyn huffed.

"Just because one Ancient One thinks we shouldn't exist doesn't make it so." Kora looked up from the boat and squealed. "There it is!"

Champion of Seasons

CHAPTER TWO

Lyn spotted land on the horizon. The boat sailed towards the mass, and soon it was scraping up onto the beach. The two got out and pushed the boat up to keep it from being washed away, then walked along the beach.

Lyn spied one, then two, then dozens of golden flowers of various shapes and sizes adorning the shoreline, their petals gleaming under the sun. "This is

Champion of Seasons

Mother's land," Kora explained. "It's part of Elysium. We're close."

"Elysium?" Lyn asked, as the two found a pathway and began to follow it.

Along the way, they found more of the golden flowers. They also periodically saw people in white robes; they were all smelling flowers or sunbathing or running around meadows, sitting under trees or climbing them, or playing with various animals and insect life. The people looked like they were in a delirium, appearing elated but not knowing why.

"Those are chosen people," Kora said, "who come here to be in eternal bliss. To remain this happy, they had to forget who they were so they wouldn't be burdened by what they lost in coming here."

Champion of Seasons

"Forget..." A stricken look came over Lyn as her thoughts swung back to the five dead pilgrims, and her life with them in Mabe, and life in general. "Why? I wouldn't want to forget anything."

"Well, Lyn, there are two types of happiness," said Kora. "There's the 'I'm having the greatest of times' happiness, and there's 'the light at the end of the tunnel' happiness. These people will always experience the 'greatest of times' bliss but are robbed of the 'light at the end of the tunnel' contentment, for in order to feel the latter, you have to experience trauma. In a way, it's the more lasting form of happiness, the happiness that allows hope to flourish in the darkest of times."

Champion of Seasons

"Ah, you made it at last!" a male voice echoed behind them. The two turned around and saw a regal-looking man. He had shiny blond hair and an even, tanned complexion—one you get from being in fine summer destinations and not from having toiled the fields your whole life. His eyes were the colour of smoky quartz, and he was dressed in a bright-white robe with silver pauldrons fixed on his shoulders. An azure cape cascaded down his back from the pauldrons and trailed on the ground. His feet were encased in gold-leafed sandals. On his fingers were rings of many metals and gemstones, and he had an amulet of a double axe around his neck in soft gold, as well as golden ear clips. His eyes narrowed on Lyn. "Who are you?" he asked. "You clearly aren't from around here."

"Oh, she's with me," Kora answered. "This is Lyn. She escorted me here from —"

"Didn't he send a guard with you?" the man interjected. "I know your mother has a low opinion of him, but I know better! He loves you very much, and he would protect you so you would come back to him."

"Of course he sent guards, Rhada. You're completely right about him," Kora replied. "But the guards were all ambushed and killed, leaving me on my own. It was dreadful!"

"I see..." His eyes narrowed further. "You poor girl indeed," he stated in monotone. He then softened his expression. "Well, the important thing is you're alive and you've come back to see your mother. She'll be thrilled, as will most of Elysium. Everyone here looks forward to your return, and there will be a party in your honour."

"Wonderful." Kora smiled. "You know, Rhada, Lyn here is strong! I mean, she defeated a kraken!"

"I really wasn't that—" Lyn began before Rhada interrupted with, "Really? A kraken? I wonder what the sea king thinks of this. Still, impressive!"

"I know, and she and I fought a yeti!" Kora smiled again.

"Yes...that happened too," Lyn replied uneasily. Would this man take what Kora's contribution to the fight was well?

Champion of Seasons

"Sounds exciting." Rhada grinned. "Well, don't let me hold you up. Your mother is waiting, you know."

"It's good to talk to you, as always," Kora replied before walking off, gesturing for Lyn to follow.

They walked along a path lined with vivid flowers and healthy-looking trees. Sitting naked under a tree was a woman who appeared to have skin made of bark. When she saw the two passing by, she leapt to her feet. "Oh, by the gods! *It's you!*" the woman shrieked. "We must tell Mother!" The strange woman gave Kora a hug, which Kora received excitedly and comfortably. The woman then unfolded orange-and-black butterfly wings and flew off down the path.

Champion of Seasons

Awestruck, Lyn turned to stare at Kora. "Who *are* you?" she asked again.

"I am Kora, I told you. And we're almost at Mother's!"

Lyn took a breath, and the two began walking. "Who was that?" she asked.

"Oh, that's Willow. She's a nymph."

"A nymph..." Lyn repeated slowly. "You have an interesting family, given that your mother lives with nymphs."

Eventually the two approached a high dense hedge, with an opening for the path to pass through. They entered and found themselves inside a hedge maze. The hedges were tall, about eight feet, and were the greenest green. "I know the way through," Kora said. "The maze is here to confuse people who shouldn't be here."

Champion of Seasons

They walked on, Kora navigating the various turns and corners within the snaking, forking path. They walked through aisle after passage after path until they found a flower bed with a giant statue of a woman carved from an oak tree in the center. The woman looked similar to Kora, only she was older and appeared more severe, wearing plain robes with her hair down and twined with flowers and branches. A stone bench allowed an audience to view the spectacle of the statue and the vivid flowers within the bed.

Kora and Lyn took a seat. "Let's rest a little." Kora grinned. "We've been walking a while, and Mother won't die waiting an extra few minutes."

Lyn took in all the sights and sounds of birds chirping, cicadas singing, and the wind blowing ever so softly. She looked back at Kora. "This place is gorgeous," she remarked. "I can't believe you actually spend time here and may have even been raised here."

"Yep," Kora said. "This is where I'm from."

"Well, it's beautiful, yet..." Lyn's awe transformed into sorrow. "Yet my friends won't see this. They died wanting to see God in his temple, and here I am in this...paradise." A tear ran down her face. "It feels wrong."

"It's not," Kora replied, putting an arm around Lyn.

"Why...why *me*?" Lyn grabbed her face and began to cry, her sobs muffled in her hands.

Champion of Seasons

"Just because," Kora replied, rubbing Lyn's back.

"They won't even feel the sunlight on their faces again."

"You will and are," Kora said.

"It's not fair."

"Fate is never fair," Kora replied with a pained expression. "Fate takes mothers from children all the time, and feeds babies to monsters, and gets people beaten and girls raped, carrying the seed of a man they don't know and who never loved them. It burns houses and melts steel. It makes farmland barren and floods vast cities. Fate is far from fair—it's cruel and acts on a whim no one understands, not even gods."

Lyn took a deep breath. "Sorry, Kora. I—"

Champion of Seasons

Kora cut her off. "No, it's okay. Just let it out. Let it all out."

A few minutes later, Lyn wiped the tears from her face with her sleeve. "I'm ready," she said.

The two kept walking past beds full of blooms of various colours and shapes before they eventually found a door that led out of the maze.

Kora opened the door, and the two walked through it. On the other side, they found rows and rows of manicured gardens with every flower that was ever known to exist and many more that no one knew existed, as far as the eye could see. In the center of all this, they found a strange structure that appeared to be a hut made of wood surrounded by a moat fed by a river behind it. The hut was connected to a bridge that led to hedges with doors and views of the sky overhead.

Lyn pointed to the hut. "Your mother lives there?"

"Her house extends to those hedges over there, each acting as a room within a larger structure," Kora explained.

As the two walked, they saw three more nymphs. One was blue with gills, and one was green with smooth skin and a bud on her forehead. The third was the nymph they saw before—the one with skin made of bark. As Lyn and Kora approached, the nymphs squealed in glee. A moment later, a woman emerged from the hut. She looked like the statue of the woman in the hedge maze: she had bright auburn hair with branches twined into the braids and was dressed in a simple robe.

Champion of Seasons

She had bright green eyes and looked like an older version of Kora.

"Mommy!" Kora rejoiced as she approached the older woman and threw her arms around her.

As the two embraced, a slight smile crept onto Lyn's face. The nymphs cheered in excitement. "Told you!" the bark-skinned nymph said.

Kora's mother pulled away from her daughter. "Where is his entourage?" she asked. "Don't tell me that ghoul made you come here by yourself!"

"We were ambushed, Mother. I was the only survivor. Lyn here escorted me."

Kora's mother sighed. "Of course he sent his worst guards. What do you expect from him?" She sneered before her expression softened. "Still, thank you,

Champion of Seasons

Lyn, for safeguarding my daughter. Please stay for the night. We'll be celebrating her return, and you should be part of that."

"That would be nice, but—" Lyn started before Kora interrupted her.

"Oh, Mother. That's so kind of you! Lyn would very much love to stay! Right, Lyn? Live a little? Be happy?"

"Seta, prepare one of the guest rooms for this woman," the older Kora directed the plant nymph.

The nymph nodded. "Of course! Anything for your daughter's champion!"

"Champion..." Lyn repeated uneasily.

Daylight faded into night as the two entered a field that had been prepared with various food and drink. Lyn kept to herself

Champion of Seasons

as she sampled cooked meats, steamed vegetables, breads, pastries, fruit juices, wines, ciders, and beers.

"Whoa, was it hard?" a gruff squeak came from behind Lyn. She turned around to see a short man with ram horns on his head, hooved goat-like feet, and brown fur along his barely clothed body—a satyr. "Hard when you formed from the sea foam?" the curious creature continued with a mischievous smirk.

"Uh...I didn't ..." Lyn gave a confused response before the satyr replied with a smile.

"Oh, I know you came from the sea—word has it you brought Kora over the sea to get here, and you sure as the grass grows under the sun look like you were formed from the foam of the sea itself."

Champion of Seasons

"I wasn't, though," Lyn replied, taking a step back from the little man.

"Oh, that's difficult to believe," the satyr replied. "You look so beautiful!" He gave a twirled bow and took a step forward.

"Pippin, leave her be," bellowed a deeper, gruffer male voice.

Lyn looked over to see a creature that, from the waist up, was a very chiseled man with a braided beard and a necklace made of teeth; from the waist down, he was a horse—a centaur. "It's obvious you're too small for her. She wants a *man*, Pip, one with length and girth," the half horse chided.

"Uh..." Lyn replied uneasily as she took another step back.

Champion of Seasons

"Name's Mortin, by the way," the centaur said, "and no one told me how smokin' the champion would be! Wow. You look like you could use a good ride, and believe me, I know a thing or two about *rides*."

"Typical centaur," Pippin quipped. "So gauche! I mean, just 'cuz I'm small doesn't mean I don't know what I'm doing! I can take you on a better tour than this oaf who thinks he just needs to put it out there!"

"It's a fact: bigger is better," Mortin retorted, looking at Lyn more than Pippin. "And you know what they say about stallions!"

Lyn took another step back. "Gentlemen, no disrespect... I'm just not in the mood," she said, turning her attention to one of the tables of food.

"All right..." Pippin looked downtrodden. "I'm not far away if you change your mind! I will blow your mind."

"I'll be with those nymphs," Mortin stated, "if you change your mind, though it'll be a short window if you want to be my only mare for the night."

The two men (creatures?) left in different directions. Lyn went to look for a quieter place, one where she could just watch the spectacle before her.

However, it was hard to keep a low profile among flirtatious satyrs and centaurs, as well as the giggling nymphs and dryads who all knew Lyn as Kora's champion. A fact that was made clear when several nymphs approached her. "Oh, champion! Come, dance!" said a nymph with small vines growing from her head as she made a gentle grab for Lyn's arm.

Lyn broke away. "No, thank you. I'd rather not. "

"Aw, why not?" another nymph stated, this one with translucent skin and white hair that appeared to be blowing in a wind far stronger than there really was. "Why be alone at such a merry time! The time of spring! Of warmth!"

"I just want to be alone," Lyn replied, backing away. "I've lost too much and I'm only here out of respect for—"

"Oh, no! The Fates were unkind to you!?" A small sprite with butterfly wings, green skin, and black compound eyes gawked in horror. "Everyone! Group hug!"

Lyn couldn't resist the various nymphs and sprites as they wrapped their arms around her, nuzzling close, cooing words of comfort. She let out a sigh as she surrendered to the attention. Not a moment passed before a walking tree wrapped a branch around them and smaller animals of the woods and grasslands gathered.

"Come on. Let's dance!" a blue nymph with gills called out.

Lyn finally smiled as the group held hands to form a circle and danced to music provided by a band of sprites and satyrs. Eventually they broke away, and Lyn went back to watching the other partiers as they all ate, drank, and danced.

Champion of Seasons

Of course, Kora was among them, playing with the nymphs in a jovial fashion, laughing as she chased and was chased by them, and made angels in the long grass and danced in circles. The night was starting to wind down, and some of the partiers were falling asleep, conversing about issues Lyn had no knowledge of and engaging in sexual behaviour, thinking no one saw them (some were more successful than others of course).

At the darker end of the night, Lyn decided to retire. As she walked to the room she was shown earlier, she passed the hut, where the window was open. She overheard the older woman say, "Has he hurt you?"

"No, Mother," Kora replied in a bored tone. "We've been through this. We

Champion of Seasons

go through this every time I come back home. No, he's never laid a hand on me in anger or so much as raised his voice to me. He's a good man."

"Oh, come off that," Kora's mother barked. "I know the stories about him and his people, about men in his echelon! How they run around violating every hole they can find and throw violent tantrums all around!"

"Yes, his 'brothers' are like that," Kora retorted. "Not him, though. He's different—he's quiet and reserved and a little shy. He's so sweet! I know how his brothers act. One of them threw a fit when we sailed over there."

"Ugh, the thought of you having to go back there sickens me." Kora's mother made a gagging sound.

Champion of Seasons

"Mother, he does what he does because someone has to," Kora replied. "He isn't defiling bodies. He's honouring them as they're supposed to be. It's very noble actually."

Lyn walked on; this conversation was none of her business. Weary, she wanted some sleep before she embarked on her journey home. She found her "room"—a sectioned-off part of a hedge maze that had a wooden door to forbid entry and a roof that was open to the sky. It held a wooden bed that was fluffed with fine sheep's wool and down feathers. Lyn lay on her back and looked up to the night sky. It was clear and all the stars were visible, showing off the constellations and the stories the stars happily told.

Champion of Seasons

Sleep didn't come to Lyn readily. She could only think of the dead pilgrims she'd had to leave behind on the mountain and how they would never see anything remotely close to this. None of the beauty of this place, or any other place, like the temple of the High God.

Suddenly there was a knock on Lyn's door. "Come in," she called out.

The door opened to reveal the smiling face of Kora, who closed the door behind her and slumped down on the grass floor. "How is my 'champion' doing?" she asked with a giddy smile.

"I'm okay."

"No, you're not okay. What's wrong?"

"I can't get them out of my head," Lyn replied. "I look at the beauty and majesty of this place, and I shouldn't be able to. I should be dead. Dead like the others: Father Triff, Ella, Jason, Paige, and Del. I shouldn't have seen *any* of this beauty. I shouldn't have—"

"Yeah, you should. That's silly," Kora said. "You survived. Why does it matter? You're alive! You should be happy! Come on, this is getting old. Think about it: you were in a very, very cold place and had to run from a monster. You hid in a cave and you found a scared girl. You got out and you fought the monster and climbed down the mountain! Lyn, you are alive and you are strong! Thrive! If not for you, for them! See what they cannot see. Learn what they cannot learn. Experience what they cannot experience. Live to honour them."

Champion of Seasons

Lyn was quiet for a moment. She thought about what Kora had said. To live for her fellow pilgrims. She looked at the hedge uneasily.

Kora broke the silence. "Do you have a mother?"

"I do. She lives in Mabe."

"Would you want to be able to embrace her again," said Kora, "and not have her wondering what happened to you? Oh! What about the families of the pilgrims? I think Jason's parents would want to know of the fate that befell him, as would Ella's. What of Paige's husband and her children and grandchildren? Or Father Triff's order and congregation? The mercenary group Del reports to? Shouldn't they know one of their fine soldiers won't be coming back? If you all

Champion of Seasons

had died, no one would ever know what fate befell the six of you. Because you survived, at least their deaths won't be a mystery to them—they'll be spared wondering where they are and what happened to them. Lyn, your life is a divine gift for them. You can at least give them closure."

A tear escaped Lyn's eye. "You're right, I guess," she uttered. "I just never expected my life to go like this."

"Most of life is unplanned, no matter how orderly we try to make it. You need to know when to roll with it and when to act. Either way, live without regret."

"I guess," Lyn said reluctantly.

"No...no, you *know*," Kora replied with a grin.

Champion of Seasons

She excused herself, leaving Lyn to gaze at the stars. The vastness of the sky always made her feel so small, so helpless among the cosmos. Lyn's life was but a drop in that bucket, her choices only mattering so much within the greater scheme of things. On that thought, she drifted off to sleep.

In the morning, she awoke to a gentle knock on the door. She opened it to find Kora's smiling face on the other side. "Wakey-wakey! It's time!" Kora beamed as Lyn followed her out and walked among the beauties of the fields and lush hedges, observing many a woodland spirit overcoming the exertion of the affairs and drink of the night prior. As the two strolled to the meeting hall to grab breakfast before heading for the shore, they gawked at drunk satyrs and exhausted nymphs. The hall was a mess full of dishevelled fairies and hungover centaurs.

"Look at all this," Kora told Lyn between bites of pancake. "Living life without worry or care."

"Yeah," Lyn replied. "They sure partied hard."

"Long into the night." Kora smiled. "They do this whenever I come home...and to a minor degree throughout the year."

Lyn smiled too. "Sounds like a fun time."

"Oh, you're smiling!" Kora smirked mischievously. "Look at that! From ear to ear!" Lyn giggled in embarrassment. "It's

Champion of Seasons

such a thing of beauty to see on you. Eh, learning to be happy!"

"Yeah, yeah!" Lyn giggled, finding no way to contain the sudden burst of joy.

"You're going to be okay," Kora said.

When the two finished up, they made their way along the path before finding their way to the shore, where the boat was waiting with a river nymph sitting at the helm.

There was a small procession of nymphs, dryads, and strange trees the dryads were riding. The two approached, and there was a small eruption of cheering as they came. Standing on the shore was Kora's mother, holding a yellow orb the size of a watermelon. The cheering died down as the powerful woman of this

Champion of Seasons

strange realm pointed to Lyn. "Champion, approach!" she commanded.

Confused, Lyn looked to Kora. "Just go. It'll be fine," Kora encouraged.

Lyn walked up, and the nymphs and fairies all stood as she approached. Lyn stood in front of Kora's mother and instinctively went down on one knee.

"Lyn, champion of my daughter! I want you to take this with you as a token of thanks. It will be something you will need in future times," she said.

Lyn got a better look at the orb: it looked like a severed eyeball with a yellow iris and a frog-like pupil. Wedged through it was a sword, a simple iron weapon Lyn immediately recognized.

"We found a deceased kraken on our shores," Kora's mother continued, "with a

Champion of Seasons

gouge in its eye—a gouge made with this weapon. This eye is yours and deserves to be returned to you." Nodding, Lyn took it from Kora's mother. "Rejoice! My child is home because of her champion! Rejoice!" All the audience, including Kora, cheered wildly. As they did so, Kora's mother put an arm around Lyn. "Your mother is still alive?" she asked Lyn.

"Aye, ma'am," Lyn replied.

"You go to her. She must be worried sick, especially if you've been gone for a while." She gave Lyn a worried look. "I know I wouldn't want to miss my Kora for any real length of time. I'm sure your mother feels the same way."

Lyn gave a nod in solidarity. She knew her mother wanted the best for her and indeed would worry if no word came

Champion of Seasons

of her safe arrival to the temple. After all, her mother did push her to make this trip in the first place.

She boarded the ship, then turned to wave at Kora and the gathering of woodland folk as they sailed away. Lyn spent the trip sitting quietly, staring out into the vast connecting sea, the sentiment bittersweet. While the detour with Kora had been filled with fantastical vistas, the trip was otherwise a waste of time. The pilgrimage had failed, and her ultimate goal of getting to the High Temple to start training as a nun had failed with it. Still, she was alive—that was all she could show for her empty hands.

The voyage went smoothly. Land was soon reached, and Lyn thanked the water fairy as she turned and walked along

Champion of Seasons

the trail back to Mabe with her tail between her legs and a dead man's sword on her hip.

Champion of Seasons

CHAPTER THREE

As Lyn strolled through the small village of her childhood, she noted all the trappings of the spring festival. She wore a small smile—after all, the pilgrimage had been timed so she would have ended up missing this. Roses, violets, forget-me-nots, morning glories, and dandelions had been strung up all over the village center, where the mayor's manor was located. Lyn saw the scaffolding where homemade decorations, wreaths, and blossoms had

Champion of Seasons

been hung. Spring was here, and all the villagers seemed excited; the buzz within the village was inescapable. Lyn was happy to be home even if the sights paled in comparison to those in Elysium.

She found the home made of lumber built on masoned stone she shared with her mother. As Lyn opened the door and walked in, she saw a robust woman with Lyn's blond hair going gray, and her blue eyes. Her mother was wearing a faded brown dress with a worn cotton apron on it. Lyn approached the older woman, who loomed over a cauldron. The smell of boiling peas and pork filled the air.

"Mom," Lyn softly spoke.

Her mother leapt as though Lyn had shouted, then approached her and gave

Champion of Seasons

her a giant hug. "Oh, Lyn, my girl!" she nearly shrieked. "You're back so soon!"

"Yeah, I know," Lyn replied in a sombre tone. "The pilgrimage failed. I was lucky to have survived."

"Survived?" Lyn's mother gave her a strange look. "What do you mean?"

"Every...everyone died." Lyn let a tear fall down her face.

"What?!" Her mother's eyes went wide. "The rest of them? But I thought you had hired muscle with you?"

"He's dead too," Lyn replied. "We were on Mount Kikica and—"

"What were you doing there?" Her mother's jaw dropped. "That place is dangerous!"

"Father Triff had the idea that it would shorten the pilgrimage," Lyn

Champion of Seasons

explained. "But there was an avalanche, and we were attacked by a yeti, and I was the only one to get away from it." She slumped onto a chair in the kitchen. "In a way, I wish I had died with them."

"Oh, no, don't say that," her mother countered. "I'm sure what happened was dreadful, but honey, you came home to me. Eh? That's what matters."

Lyn sat there quietly, Kora's words from last night turning in her head.

"I have some pork stew bubbling," Lyn's mother said with a smile. "Would you like a bowl?"

Lyn nodded and shared the food with her mother. The stew tasted as her mother always made it, with home and hearth in the center of it all. During the meal, Lyn told her about her adventures

Champion of Seasons

with Kora, how she found the girl in the cave and how they fended off the yeti, then bandits, and a kraken in the sea, and how they met fairies in a large garden.

Her mother was surprised, horrified, amazed, excited, and in disbelief. "Well, it explains the sword, Lyn," she said. "I mean, I understand you needed to defend yourself, but it's such an unladylike thing to have, and you won't need it when you become a nun of the High God!"

"Well, Mom..." Lyn grew solemn, then mustered up her courage and said, "I'm not sure I want to be a nun."

"Don't say things like that," her mother replied in shock. "You've always wanted to be a nun! I was so worried that bastard boy was going to take that away from you!"

Champion of Seasons

"No, Mom. *You* wanted this for me," Lyn responded. "You've always commented on how pretty and virtuous the nuns are and how I could become one so I could be educated, and sheltered from harm, and to make sure a boy never took me away from you. I was doing all this for you. I was on that pilgrimage for *you*, to make you proud of me."

"Lyn, I understand what happened was awful," her mother said softly, "but that's the best possible life you could have! You'd never need to depend on a man and you'd be protected."

"What of family and children? What of romance and lovemaking?"

"Romance is overrated, honey," her mother retorted. "It's good for making bastard kids and that's it! It isn't like the men stay or nothing!"

"Didn't you love Father?"

"Your father left us, the asshole!" her mother snarled.

"Mom, he died in the battle of the Holy Fire in Urot," Lyn shot back.

"As for family…" her mother began then grew quiet.

"What of family?" Lyn growled with the understanding that she had trapped her mother. "What's wrong with wanting to wake up in the morning to your husband and your kids, who are happy to see you alive?"

"That's a fairy tale. It's a hard life, one I would like you to avoid. I would love you to be happy without that burden."

Champion of Seasons

"So I'm a burden." Lyn scowled. "Thanks, Mom."

"That's not what I meant. I just…" Her mother looked like she was vibrating with rage. "I want what's best for you; I want you to have the easiest possible life. Now you can stay as long as you need." She began to calm herself. "You can go out on another pilgrimage when you're ready, but you'll give up that blasted blade. Women do not need it!"

"Can't I keep it as a memento?" Lyn asked with doe eyes, burying her anger, as she had been during this conversation. "I promise not to wear it. It'll be in my room or in my pack."

Lyn's mother thought deeply. "Fine," she replied. "You can keep that blasted thing!"

Champion of Seasons

Lyn's return to Mabe did bring a stir. Word had been going around about her exploits, with a few people prying at her as she went about her business. Some doubted her tale as hallucinations and hyperbole, while others were excited to the point of talking about her bringing down giants and dragons. None of which had happened, but many felt she should be larger than life, her tale more fantastical than it already was.

One by one, Lyn made her rounds. She started with the church. Inside, she found Father Gommit at the altar, preparing his sermon. He was a middle-aged man with a sturdy build and balding brown hair. "Lyn, back so soon?" he asked. Lyn nodded while looking at her

Champion of Seasons

shoes. "It's good to see a member of the flock back, but what is the matter?"

"Father Triff, he's—" Lyn choked on her words. "He's dead... They're all dead."

Father Gommit walked down from the altar and placed a hand on Lyn's shoulder. "It's all right, child. I... understand," he said quietly, sombrely.

At that moment a nun came in, carrying the eucharist. "Is something wrong, Father?"

"It's Father Triff," he replied. "He isn't coming home. This girl was on his pilgrimage."

"No!" the nun screamed. "What happened?"

"We were on Mount Kikica," Lyn recited. "And there was an avalanche, and

Champion of Seasons

then we were attacked by a yeti. I barely got out alive."

"By the High God, Father Triff was the head of the church!" The nun further panicked. "What will we do now?"

"We will do as we must," Father Gommit replied. "And a memorial will be held for Father Triff and the rest of the pilgrims."

"You wretched child!" the nun lunged for Lyn, only for Father Gommit to grab her and hold her still. She thrashed in vain as Father Gommit growled, "Sister Gwendoline, pull yourself together! She's just the messenger!" Sister Gwendoline stopped thrashing and Father Gommit let her go. "I need to pray," she whimpered as she walked towards the back room of the church.

Champion of Seasons

Father Gommit turned to Lyn. "Unless there's anything further, you are dismissed. Be with God, my child."

Next Lyn made her way to a quaint cottage on the outskirts of the village. The home was made of stone and wood and had a oak door that looked worn with age. Lyn gave it a knock. Moments later a woman in a white habit with a cross pendant opened the door, her grey eyes looking at Lyn expectantly.

"Hello, is this where Ella, the vestal in training, lived...lives?" Lyn asked.

"It is, miss. Can I help you?" the woman replied in a curious tone.

"It's about her," Lyn said, her tone solemn "I'm afraid to tell you she has passed on."

"Oh..." The woman broke down in tears. "That is—was—my daughter...no." She turned around. "Herbert," she called out. "Ella has died."

"What?" An older gentleman came to the door and looked at Lyn. His brown eyes held a degree of malice, and he wore the vestments of a layman. "How did that happen?"

"We were on Mount Kikica and were attacked..." Lyn began before the man interjected with "Mount Kikica? Oh, High God, keep Ella's pure soul safe." As he closed the door, the sound of wailing escaped the house.

After that, Lyn visited the bakery, located in the stone building in the center of town. The kindly old man who ran the

Champion of Seasons

place was burly with a white beard that covering his wrinkled, tanned face.

"Lyn!" he exclaimed. "Back so soon? And how is Paige fairing?"

"Ben, I'm sorry." She bowed her head. "The pilgrimage was a failure. I was the..." She choked on her words. "I was the only survivor. Paige is dead. Again, I'm so sorry."

"Oh..." Ben bowed his head.

A tense silence ripped through the bakery. Lyn broke the silence with, "She took care of all of us during the pilgrimage."

"I-I'm sure she did," Ben said, still gathering himself from the blow. He slumped onto a stool by the oven, looked to Lyn, and said, "Please go."

Lyn nodded and walked away.

Champion of Seasons

On the outskirts of Mabe stood a large house, the largest she had ever seen, with wood and masonry holding it all together. She knocked on the door to the manor and waited. The door opened to an old man in a black suit who looked at her as though he were bored. "Is this where Jason lives?" she asked him.

"It is," the man replied. "But I'm afraid he's away and won't be back for a while."

The man was about to shut the door when Lyn spoke up. "I came to see his parents, not him."

He looked back to Lyn. "Wait," he said, then closed the door. His footfalls broke through as Lyn stood patiently in the warm sun. After some time, he returned, opened the door, and gestured

Champion of Seasons

Lyn inside. "This way, miss, to the master of the house."

She followed without protest. The man led her through halls of red carpet with plaster trim and portraits everywhere to a den painted in a red dye. Seated in a throne-like chair was a well-dressed man with a purple sash. He was fat and had some grey in his hair.

"You wish to seat audience with me?" he asked impatiently.

"Yes..." Lyn looked him in the eyes. "It's about your son, Jason."

"He was sent on a pilgrimage the temple of the High God!" he roared. "What could he possibly have done?"

"Mi'lord, he's...dead." Lyn shook as she answered.

Champion of Seasons

"Dead? Dead!" his annoyance gave in to rage. "How? He was with the best of the High God in the region!"

"We were on Mount Kikica and—" Lyn started, only for Jason's father to interrupt with, "In winter? What in the hells were you thinking?! I'm going after the church for this...this..." Tears came over him in his fury.

"As you wish, mi'lord," Lyn responded. "I just came to deliver the news. I shall be off."

"Please," Jason's father spat as the doorman escorted her from the house.

Lastly she went to the postman with a note for the Troupe of the Flaming Shield—the mercenary group Del was from. The note read thus:

Champion of Seasons

To the Flaming Shield,

I regret to inform you that Del of the Shield died in battle, carrying out his duties. He was killed by a monster on Mount Kikica, defending the people he was paid to protect. Please forward this news to any family he has.

Sincerely yours,
Lyn of Mabe

She handed the letter to the postman in a busy building in the heart of Mabe, explaining to a tired man in plain linen where she wanted it to go. He nodded and stacked it accordingly.

As deeply saddening as this all was, it also filled Lyn with a strange sense of

Champion of Seasons

purpose: Kora was right—she had she lived to tell others their loved ones had passed on.

That week, Lyn got a job at the bakery to keep herself out of the house and help support her mother. The spring festival went as expected, with various contests and the major's typically embarrassing speech. Lyn kept to herself but still walked around to soak in the sights.

A few days after the festival, she was doing her job at the bakery—mixing dough in the heat of the spring weather—when they ran out of flour.

"We can't have this," Ben panicked. "Lyn! Take the cart and this pouch and go to the mill!"

Champion of Seasons

Lyn didn't need to look inside to know there were gold coins in the pouch. She nodded and embarked.

That was where she met *him*. Partway to the mill, as she pulled the cart towards, she passed a guard on duty. She had seen him around before, with a shy look in his green eyes when he was looking at her. She caught his gaze and a blush spread across his olive face. An embarrassed smile rose high in his cheeks and poked out from the hardened leather of his helmet—protection against soldiers, beasts, and criminals, but not pretty ladies, it seemed.

"Sorry, ma'am. I...I wasn't meaning to..." he said when Lyn stopped. Despite having a body forced into fitness from his work, he looked winded. "I mean, I was...

Champion of Seasons

Yeah... I was just keeping watch... Ah, I feel like I should know you."

"Guardsman, are you all right?" Lyn replied. "You look like you're about to faint. Need water? I'm heading for the miller. The river isn't far and I have a spare bottle."

"No, no... It's okay. I...like..." the guard stammered. "I'm being awkward, ma'am—I am. Sorry."

"You sure you'll be okay?" Lyn asked with some concern. "I'm Lyn, by the way."

"Really?" The guard looked excited, like a famous bard had just spoken to him. "*The* Lyn? I've heard stories about you around town. Is it true you slayed a yeti?"

"I had help with that one," she said quietly. "I was with a..." What exactly was

Champion of Seasons

Kora? "Well, she had magicks that helped, yeah." *Let's not tell people she raised the dead.*

"Still, you dealt the killing blow!" He had a sparkle in his eyes. "And did you fight a kraken too?"

"I got lucky with the kraken. I threw my blade at it, and the beast sank into the sea. Even got the blade later when it came up on shore."

"Oh, goodness! You're pretty *and* brave..." The guard's excitement died in his throat at the realization he had just said that out loud. "I...mean, like, you had, like, valour. I-I'm sorry; I really am. I'm being creepy, I know."

A smile crept onto Lyn's face. "Well, I'm afraid I'm on the clock," she pointed out. "I need to get this cart to the miller—

the baker needs flour. We can talk later, okay?"

"Oh...my...gods ..." The guard shook his head and stood upright. "I mean, yeah, I would like that. Name's Rothan by the way." Lyn gave him a wink before continuing on her way.

At the miller's, she handed over the pouch and asked for flour, and the miller took it and filled the cart with the sacks. She pulled the cart back to the gate, noting that Rothan was no longer on the corner where she had met him.

Shame, how often in this village, or anywhere, men went nuts over a woman with a sword. Lyn thought this was strange and would have loved to see the boy awkwardly squirm some more before breaking it to him that she was human too.

Champion of Seasons

The next morning, she walked by the same area before her shift started at the bakery, and she found him. He stood there, leaning against a pillar like he'd been there for a while. The street was quiet. Lyn walked up with a smile. "Rothan?" she asked, stopping a few feet from him. His face lit up at the sight of her. "I'm sorry I missed you after I came out of the miller's yesterday," she continued. "I didn't realize I'd caught you at the end of your shift."

"Oh...it's okay," Rothan replied, straightening himself. "You had no way of knowing I was on the weird bewitching shift and you'd caught me near the end."

"You work all night then?" Lyn asked.

Champion of Seasons

"Yep. As you know, someone has to."

"Crime doesn't sleep, I suppose," Lyn replied. "I mean, I feel safer knowing you're at the ready in the dead of night."

"Oh, but you don't need a guard," Rothan continued. "I mean, you can, like, fight and use, like, a sword!"

"Well, I'm not armed anymore," Lyn said. "I mean, I took the sword from a dead man's grip out of desperation, and it's unladylike to carry such weapons around."

"So you had to get rid of the sword?" A look of sadness came over him. "I mean, it sounded like you were a natural."

"Well, I convinced my mother to let me keep it as a memento," Lyn said. "So I still have it. 'Course I can't exactly carry it around."

"Well, why can't—" Rothan's words died in his throat. If anyone overheard him, there would be much judgement from the village, as weapons were things men possessed, and women were to cling to strong men who could look after themselves. Rothan looked at his shoes, then back at Lyn. "Can...can I admit something?" he asked.

Lyn walked to within whispering range of him. "What?" she asked with a quiver in her voice. *He's not going to tell me he loves me, is he?* she thought. *I mean, we just met, for the love of Petra!*

"I wish women didn't have to be so dainty," Rothan confessed. "I mean, it's just...something about a woman shrieking over a mouse, or running and hiding behind some beefy man, or being completely helpless in the dark... I just find it all a turn-off. I want a strong, no-nonsense girl, you know?" He gave Lyn a faint smile. "One who can walk beside me, who has my back as much as I have hers, to see the world with. You can't see the world with a fragile flower who freaks out at the first sight of blood."

Lyn gave him a queer stare. "Don't you want a pretty girl who would tidy the house, bake pies, and watch your kids?" she asked. *Weird man.*

"I would like to think I could hire a maid, cook, and nanny if that's all I wanted," he replied. "I don't want to marry someone just to get a cheap servant

I can also take to bed... That's prostitution, if you think about it."

"I gotta get going," Lyn said continuing towards the bakery, pondering Rothan's words.

That night, after her shift and after she finished eating dinner, Lyn crawled underneath the covers of her down mattress. Propped against the wall on the other side of the room was the sword she'd grabbed from Del's cold hands. It stood there reminding her of the challenges and the odd sights and sounds she'd experienced with Kora, a once-in-a-lifetime journey that wouldn't repeat itself.

As she drifted off, she remembered Rothan's words. Surely he couldn't be the only man who felt that way, right? Of course, Lyn couldn't call herself unique for having been through what she had; she was sure plenty of people had adventures. Still, society had expectations for her. Her mother had expectations for her. And Rothan had his duties, even if he was being weird.

The next day, Lyn ran into Rothan in the same spot as before. He looked at her like he wanted to say something. Lyn stopped and waited.

"Lyn, I don't know how you feel about me...and...I guess I acted strangely again and—" he stammered.

"It's fine," Lyn replied, "though I don't know if I'm the girl you're looking for. I mean, I did what I did to survive, not because I wanted to. I'm studying to be a nun; I was on that pilgrimage to become one."

"You slew a kraken and you want to be a nun?" Rothan asked in confusion. "I mean, if that's what you want. But from what little I know, you're better than that."

"It's what my mother wants," Lyn replied.

"Is it what you want?"

"I need to get running, Rothan," she said, looking towards the bakery.

"We should...should be friends."

Lyn smiled. "I agree. I shall see you later."

They fell into a routine of chatting in the wee hours of the morning, the only time

Champion of Seasons

Lyn could find Rothan conveniently. Talking to him was a refreshing break from her mundane days of preparing for a life she might not really want.

One day, Rothan made an offer. "Lyn, I really don't want you to give up the way of the blade—you seem so natural at it. Why don't I show you how to use the sword better? I have a soldier's martial training, and I could use practice teaching."

It was a bold offer indeed. He effectively was asking her to go against much of what society had taught her regarding what being a woman meant while spending extended periods of time alone with a man in the woods. This was something that gave Lyn much pause. In the end, what swayed her was how Rothan made her feel about herself—how he seemed enamoured by qualities she'd never thought she possessed and wasn't put off by her at all. Perhaps she could get more time with him before the bubble about her burst and he saw her for the human she really was and not this...hero?

"Yes, I'll do it," she said after an uneasy pause.

The two agreed to train before Rothan's shift began and after her shift ended. Every morning Lyn went off to the bakery, sneaking the sword in a pack she used for her lunch and shopping. She then left after work and found Rothan in a clearing in the nearby woods—their spot—where he showed her how to pose with a blade and drilled her on stances, swings, parrying, break falling, and rolling with a

Champion of Seasons

blade. She even began to build enough muscle to hold the sword in one hand for short periods of time.

The days she spent with Rothan brought them closer together, and the day she was dreading loomed closer. Her mother had given her an ultimatum: she'd force her out of the house if she didn't agree to go on the next pilgrimage to the temple of the High God that autumn. It further didn't help matters when Rothan brought up something unexpected at one of their sessions.

"Before you go for the night, can I say something?" he asked as they began to cool down.

"What is it?" Lyn asked him with a tired smile.

Champion of Seasons

"Lyn…I…I love you," he said solemnly. "I love you and it hurts, knowing you'll become a nun and you can't be with me."

"I'm sorry," Lyn replied, a tear coming down her face. "I have to do this. It's what I need to do—for my mother and the community."

"It isn't even what you want." Rothan sighed. "I can tell you this—you took to the sword faster than some in my cohort in the army."

Lyn gave him a sore look. "What role is there for a woman with a blade?"

Rothan grew silent, for he knew she was right. "Well, I hope everything works out for you," he said, his eyes misting over.

Lyn nodded, heading home with a grim expression.

Champion of Seasons

Champion of Seasons

CHAPTER FOUR

It was the night before Lyn would meet the new pilgrims. She sat in the same clearing where she usually trained with Rothan, but he was sick and wasn't giving lessons that night. She pondered her future, thinking about who she wanted to be and what she wanted to do. She considered what she must do and how she was going to do it. She had a lot on her mind and dreaded what was to come.

Champion of Seasons

That was when she heard it: a raspy but eerily familiar sound. Lyn turned and saw a young woman. She wore a ripped shawl, and her auburn hair was a mess around the flower crown in her hair. She looked at Lyn with rich green eyes.

"Lyn...I need your help again," the battered woman wheezed.

Lyn knew exactly who this was. "Kora!" she exclaimed as she approached and looked around in the trees.

"I lost them...I think," Kora replied, breathing deeply. "I was attacked again. I need your assistance getting home."

"You need to get back to your mother's house?" Lyn asked.

"No, no, I'm done with my visit with Mother. Now I'm going back home."

Champion of Seasons

Lyn thought on it. "I need to go on the pilgrimage tomorrow morning," she muttered to herself. "Mother already gave me her ultimatum…" She turned to look back at Kora. It was like being back on the mountain, where her heart overrode her conviction and duty. In the dark of the night, Lyn made her decision.

"Okay. We can head out tonight," she told Kora. "Just let me tell some people so they won't miss me."

Kora nodded and sat on a nearby stump as Lyn walked into town. She approached her home to find her mother wasn't there. Lyn wasn't sure where her mother was and didn't want to waste time hunting for her. This was when she got the idea to find the guards and have one of them tell her mother what was happening;

Champion of Seasons

she didn't want her to worry. Lyn went looking for a guard when a familiar voice called, "You're out late!" She turned to see Rothan, a bit pale and clammy looking, holding on to a post. When she approached, he smelled of whiskey.

"Rothan," Lyn began, "can you do me a favour?"

He nodded. "Sure."

"Can you tell my mother I needed to run out for the night to attend to something important? It can't wait till after the pilgrimage. I need to start it now."

"What is it?" Rothan slurred angrily. "What's more important than being a nun for Mommy dearest?"

"Kora... It's Kora," Lyn replied. "She needs help getting home again."

Champion of Seasons

"Oh! Why didn't you say so!" He looked at her enthusiastically. "I mean, I had a feeling you'd be needing that sword again! You still have it, right?"

"Yeah, in my pack here." Lyn pointed. "I was anticipating practice with you."

"Lyn, you're going to apply all of what you have learned now," Rothan replied with a smile. "Make us all proud. Make *me* proud."

Lyn smiled back. "Thank you. I will." She ran off. Even half sick and half drunk, he was adorable *and* insightful.

Lyn was back on the outskirts of the village. Kora seemed better as she sat in a small patch of pink flowers Lyn could swear hadn't been there earlier. "Ready, Kora?" she asked.

"Yep!" Kora replied. "I'll lead the way!"

The two then started to walk, with Kora taking the lead and Lyn watching for anything suspicious in the brush and ditches.

"So, Lyn," Kora asked, "how's life been?"

"All right, I guess," she replied meekly. "I'm, once again, letting down my pilgrimage troupe by escorting you, and I think my mother will disown me by the end of the night, but all is well, I suppose."

"Why would darting out on a new bunch of stuck-up pilgrims let down a group of dead people?" Kora asked.

Champion of Seasons

"Well, it's bad enough that I didn't share their fate. But it's worse that I won't finish what I started with them."

"And that's a bad thing? I mean, it's your life. You can do whatever you want with it."

"it's not that easy," Lyn replied. "I mean, we have duties and responsibilities we can't just scarper. I have a duty to Mother, and I had a duty to Ella, Paige, Jason, Del, and Father Triff."

"No, you don't," said Kora. "I mean, believe me, I thought I was obligated to do everything Mother told me to do, but the truth she never wants to accept is that I don't want to be a vestal, and I'm happy with my life."

As the two walked, the leaves of the trees browned and fell, and the air grew colder—so cold the two could see their breath. They crossed a stream that was starting to freeze over, and parts of the forest floor became ice. Soon they were in a clearing with frozen crystals on the grass.

"I'm happy to live, but a piece of me will always know I should never have left that mountain," Lyn said.

"Good. We have mutual desires," a voice called out from behind them.

Lyn and Kora turned to see the bandit leader from six months prior. He stood with a scowl as his men leapt from the brush and circled the two women.

"You bitches think you can kill Goto and get away with it?" he shouted. "You ladies are in for a treat! We're going to force you down, have our ways with ya, and gut you right here, right now!" As he

Champion of Seasons

spoke, his four men stepped closer, their weapons drawn.

Kora began to channel. The trees grew and grabbed the leader, but the rest of the men were too far from the trees and shrubs, and the grass wasn't cutting it. "Your tricks won't work here, bitch!" the leader spat as he struggled. "Boys! Get 'em! They got enough holes between the two of them!"

"Lyn, I'm sorry," Kora breathed. "Here, have a boost!" Kora channelled energy into Lyn, which made Lyn feel stronger. Lyn looked at the four coming at them. Even with Kora's strange magick, they were too much. This was when she remembered something Rothan had told her: *When outnumbered, divide and conquer! Use the lay of the land to do this, and no matter what, keep fighting!"*

Lyn jumped for one bandit with a dagger, letting her blade slice into his side. He let out a yelp as another dagger-wielding bandit lunged at her. She sidestepped away from the first bandit and did a crescent step while swinging her blade at the second bandit as he accidentally stabbed a bush. The swing grazed him and he shrieked. The third one, also holding a dagger, circled Lyn, while a fourth with a crossbow took aim. Lyn made two missed swings at the circling bandit before Rothan's voice sounded again in her head: *Don't wildly swing the blade—it's a waste of your energy. Instead, wait for an opening."*

Champion of Seasons

An opening never really came as an arrow sank into Lyn's shoulder. Screaming in agony, she dropped to the ground, her sword falling. She could have just gotten back up, even though three of the men were coming right at her, but she remembered something else Rothan had told her: *When things are dire, you can perform the false surrender or fake death. This will make the enemy lower their guard if they think they bested you. Mind you, a smarter enemy won't be fooled by this.*

The three were upon her as she gritted her teeth. She looked around to see where the fourth man was. She found him, clutching his gut as he bled onto the frozen dew. He was limping to the leader in an attempt to free him. This was while the other three were standing around Lyn.

"Nice shot!" one said. "She's completely down!"

"Well, my dick is cold, and I bet she's still warm, so..." the archer said as he dropped onto his knees and put himself between Lyn's legs. "Hey! I'm first!" another of the bandits shouted. "Get off her."

"I shot her fair and square!" the archer replied indignantly. "Besides, there's another hole, you know!"

That bandit who was complaining approached Kora, who was backing up as much as she could. The injured bandit hobbled towards her as the leader cursed in the background. "You! Let our leader out or...or your friend dies!" the injured man yelled.

Champion of Seasons

"You can't kill either of us," Kora replied with a tremble in her voice. "You can't."

"Oh, yeah!" the second bandit spat while he placed the flat of his dagger onto Kora's collarbone. "Let him out or I'll make you feel real pain, if you know what I mean."

So now, instead of three on Lyn, there were only two, and one of them had just removed his protective codpiece. *Genius. Rothan was on to something about taking down dumber mobs.* The archer reached out to lift Lyn's skirt. The other bandit standing near her was doing the same when Lyn quickly sat up and jersey-pulled the archer into her head, headbutting him while her right knee struck his groin. The archer tumbled onto

Champion of Seasons

his butt, seething in pain, while Lyn rolled towards her blade, made a grab for it, and sprang onto her feet. The other bandit stood in shock as Lyn brought her sword down on him, digging the blade into his shoulder. A moment later, he fell and bled out onto the frozen dew.

The archer was still on the ground seeing stars when the other two bandits, one already hurt by Lyn's blade, took notice. The second bandit walked behind Kora and held his blade to her throat.

"Drop your sword or I'll kill her!" he called out.

"Weren't you going to kill us anyway?" Lyn roared back.

"Ah...drop it or...I will double kill her! Painfully! With my sharp..." he scatter-thought while running the flat of the dagger along Kora's collarbone.

If the enemy demands you to drop your weapon, don't do it! It's your power! Doing that makes you powerless to the enemy, and they'll do all kinds of nasty stuff to you! Rothan's voice echoed in Lyn's mind again. She saw her opportunity as the man played with his knife on Kora's body; Lyn immediately jumped and skewered the asshole in the gut! His dagger wasn't at Kora's throat, and a cut to the collarbone would be survivable.

The injured one wildly swung his dagger at Lyn. She easily side-stepped his swing then lowered her blade on him, carving out a chunk of his neck. He collapsed and bled out on the grass. This

Champion of Seasons

was when she saw the archer stand back up. Lyn raced to him as he was about to aim his crossbow. A second later, he fell to the ground with a bloody hole in his chest.

The four bandits lay dead on the grass as the leader looked on in horror. Lyn approached him with her blade drawn and trained on his neck. "Give me a reason to spare you!" she fumed.

"You bitch! How could you!" he cried.

"If you die, no more bandits will hunt us as part of some stupid vendetta you have against us," Lyn spat back.

She then swung her blade and decapitated the man.

Kora and Lyn stood over the scene. "These brats deserve to sit in Acheron for a hundred years to think over what they've done." Kora shook her head. "They're used to pilgrims and merchants, not us. Anything less and...oh, how ghastly."

"Did I just..." Lyn's eyes didn't stray from the stump that was the bandit leader's neck.

Kora placed a hand on the shaft of the arrow sticking out of Lyn's shoulder. "He brought this on himself," she said. "He wanted to live like a bandit, so he can die like one. This is as fate dictated."

"Fate?" Lyn looked disgusted. "Kora, I killed him. How does fate play into my action?"

Kora shrugged. "You were destined to slay him. That's all really. He was to die today, and it was by your hand. I helped, of course. Lyn..." She looked Lyn in the eyes "Fate can be a cruel, cruel thing, but we can affect fate. You could have spared him, and fate would have gone somewhere else. But you didn't and you'll have to live with that. It's okay, though, for he was going to hunt us until his dying breath. He asked for this and you gave him what he was asking for."

Lyn pondered this as Kora continued. "Mother admits this is the way of nature—that one creature is to die to support another in the cycle of life and death—and my man agrees, citing everyone has their time and it will come sooner or later in some fashion."

"You're right," Lyn finally said. "They got what they deserved. We're done here."

"Agreed. Their souls are in Acheron now. They can fuss about down there."

Champion of Seasons

The two ventured onward, walking past the crystalized blood and continuing along the cooling path. As they walked, Lyn let out a gasp when she saw Mount Kikica, where her old pilgrimage group died last winter.

"Are we going to the mountain?" she asked.

Kora shook her head. "Just the base of it."

"Why...why are we coming back here?" Lyn winced.

"Because we are. Relax. We'll be fine. Come on."

"It brings up memories I wish not to —"

Kora cut her off. "Lyn, you shouldn't bury it because it's painful. Let it come to you."

Champion of Seasons

Lyn followed Kora through the meadowlands to the mountain's base, where Kora led them into a cave. "You don't still wish you died here, do you?" Kora asked.

"I...I don't know." Lyn sighed. "I don't know how to feel. I'm happy to be alive, but I know I should have—"

"Like I keep telling you, you survived. Be happy about that!" Kora flashed her a smile. "I know I'm happy you lived."

The two were in a small cavern with a symbol in the shape of a jagged helmet adorned in bones carved into the stone ground. Kora walked up to it, stood in the center, and gestured Lyn to follow. Kora knelt on the stone, her auburn hair touching the ground as she knocked twice.

Champion of Seasons

There was a rumble, and the cavern suddenly sloped downward. The two kept walking down until they reached a cavern deep underground.

This cavern was massive: the ceiling was barely visible; there was sand along the floor; and Lyn heard the sound of running water. Faint eerie blue and purple lights danced across the sand.

"Kora, where are we?" Lyn asked with a fearful look.

"Oh, this is the shores of Acheron," Kora replied with a smile.

"Wait, what?" Lyn looked horrified. "Acheron! Isn't that in... Kora, what are we doing in the...Underworld?"

"Oh, my home is in here!" Kora replied simply. "We just need to walk along the beach there to get to the boatman to sail us across—"

"My God, Kora!" Lyn interrupted. "What is a nature lover like you doing living in the realm of the...dead?"

"Oh, well, one fateful day I was in the garden in Elysium..." Kora began her tale as they walked along the beach. "I was looking after the plants and the flowers and trees in Mother's garden when, despite supposedly being alone, I realized someone was watching me. I looked around at first, but whoever it was eluded me. So finally I called out, 'Don't be shy! Anyone in Elysium can be in Mother's garden.'

"And that was when I met him. He came up from a hedge oh-so shyly, with his red eyes on me, and his black hair...and

Champion of Seasons

his pale complexion—poor boy didn't see enough sun. 'I'm sorry to scare you,' he replied. 'It's just that I'm not on the best terms with your mother, but I do love what she's done to this garden! It's so wild and exotic!'

"'Well, it's my handiwork, sir,' I replied. Oh, he was sooo sweet! We talked and talked and talked! He was a smart man with all these books, and he was very much a sweet gentleman. I was telling him about the garden and about what I did, and about everything I knew about nature and animals and all that beautiful stuff. 'Course, we got into more personal topics, and I told him about being made into a vestal and how I didn't really want that life. I wanted to be part of the cycle of life

Champion of Seasons

and nature, and remaining a virgin just seemed so...antithetical to that.

"He offered to take me to his home. There, I could be the person I wanted to be and have some freedom, and again, he had a giant library. So I went with him. Although I missed Elysium and Mother, I felt freer than ever, and he was a genuine man! I mean, I was naive at the time, later learning how much trouble I could have been in with someone else. Still, I loved being with him.

"In the time I was away, my mother grew very sad and everyone was worried. So I struck a deal: I'd spend some time with Mother during the year and the rest with my husband."

Champion of Seasons

Lyn gave her a perplexed look. "You married someone from the realm of the dead?"

"Like I said, he's amazing! Tender touch too!" Kora beamed.

As they continued on, Lyn noticed the glowing lights along the beach had the shape of people. Some wandered aimlessly while others were heading in the same direction as Lyn and Kora—likely going towards the same boat. Suddenly a group of shades saw them and charged them.

"For killing us!" the shades shouted. It was the bandits Lyn had killed. She readied her blade while Kora dropped to the ground and pounded it with her fist. A black shock wave reverberated and knocked the leader and a couple of the others into the water.

Champion of Seasons

"They would have been judged to be sent to Tartarus anyway," Kora muttered. One held his hand up and approached quietly. "I... Goto..." the shade whispered. "I am sorry." He then walked away. The remaining bandits, fearing being knocked into the river, followed him. The two kept walking.

"Tell me, Lyn," Kora asked with a mischievous grin. "Any love in your life?"

"Well...there is this boy..." Lyn stammered. "No, a man. He's definitely a man. A really sweet man. Back in Mabe, he taught me how to fight."

"Oh, is that where you learned your moves?" Kora asked with a twinkle in her eyes and a smirk on her lips.

Champion of Seasons

"Yes. He heard about what I did when I took you to your mother, and he seemed weirdly enamoured by it."

"He might be attracted to strength." Kora grinned. "Not a bad thing, really."

Five more shades peacefully approached the two. They were of various shapes and sizes, and they were looking at Lyn intently.

"Lyn!" the shade of a young woman called out. "My goodness! We were looking for you!"

"Oh, Lyn, poor child, I had hoped you at least would have survived," an older man said. "I will truly weep now that I know the pilgrimage has ended with everyone dying."

Lyn looked at the shades in bewilderment as she thought of what to say before Kora spoke up. "Lyn is actually alive—she's with me."

"What!" a teenage boy responded, "Lyn! You lucky bitch! How is life treating you?"

Lyn stood there, flabbergasted. "Lyn, sweetie, you are okay, right?" an older woman cooed. "You didn't die like we did, did you?"

"Nah, she looks lively enough," a burly young man stated with a smile. "I mean... Is that my sword?"

Lyn sheathed her blade and looked at the shades with her jaw on the ground. "My goodness. How...?" she stammered.

"Well, we died and got stuck here," the older woman, Paige, said. "I went looking for the others, walking up and down the bank until I found those I

Champion of Seasons

could. I'd hoped to be alone, but I was wrong...so wrong."

"When I realized all of you had died, I felt terrible." The burly young man, Del, sighed. "I failed your group. I really did."

"It's all right, Del," Lyn finally said. "I should have joined all of you."

The five gave her near-angry looks. "Tell me you're not serious," the young woman, Ella, balked.

"Lyn, your being alive made us feel hopeful," Father Triff, responded. "We felt joyous when we couldn't find you. We worried that you did die and your mother would never have her precious girl back."

"I mean, someone had to break what happened to my mom and dad," Jason said. "And if we all died, there would have been no one to tell anyone what happened. We would have been missing! It would have destroyed my mother, and I'm sure it would have destroyed everyone else's families as well."

"I just...it didn't sit well with me to be alive while all of you died," Lyn replied, a tear falling down her face. "Why me? Why not any one of you?"

"Lyn, why should we die at all?" said Father Triff. "Why couldn't we all have survived and reached the temple of the High God, where you would become a nun and Ella a holy vestal? Paige and I would have received favour and a blessing from the High God, and Jason would have been taught discipline." Jason stuck his tongue out at that. "And...and Del would have been paid." The glare Father Triff gave Del could have sharpened daggers.

Champion of Seasons

"Besides, Lyn, we even came back to help you with the yeti," Del stated. "Something called us and we happily answered."

"It was blasted cold and it felt so...wrong," Ella added. "However, we did it and we would do it again!"

"What? They were you?" Lyn looked shocked and moved her glare to Kora, who wore a radiant smile.

"They wanted you to live," Kora reiterated. "Let that sink in."

Lyn stared down at her feet. "It's just... I really didn't want to be the survivor, to walk this world knowing I should have died."

"Do you wish death because you don't want to live with the memory of having seen us die?" Paige asked in a calm voice.

"I can't get the thought out of my head," Lyn said. "I want to push it away, but..." She broke into tears, sobbing uncontrollably. Kora stepped towards Lyn and threw her arms around her. The shades did so as well, all gathering around the weeping Lyn.

"Let it out, Lyn," Kora whispered. "Let it out. You got off the mountain; there is no crisis. You may mourn them now."

"They turned blue and...they got torn apart..." Lyn went on. The five shades and Kora all stood there, comforting her.

When Lyn finally settled down, Kora said, "Let's get to the boat. It's not far." Gently she took Lyn by the shoulder and resumed their pace.

"The boatman won't let us on board," Jason whined. "We don't have any money on us."

Lyn reached into her coin purse and handed each of her former fellow pilgrims one coin each, which she thought should be enough to cover the fare. The five looked overjoyed.

"Thank you!" Ella remarked. "We were getting bored just walking along the shore."

"Agreed. I mean, a hundred years, really?" Jason added.

The dock was made of a very dry black wood. The structure extended out to a black gondola with a robed figure standing with a paddle. The group

Champion of Seasons

approached the foreboding person, who pointed at them with an outstretched bony hand.

"One coin to cross," a very raspy male voice bellowed. "One coin or you'll wander for one hundred years."

Each of the shades paid the coin and boarded. As Lyn tried to board, the robed figure looked at her with glowing purple eyes and said, "What is a living soul doing down here?"

"Oh, Charon, she's with me!" Kora said.

"If you insist, Your Majesty," Charon replied with a raspy sigh. "You'll explain this to the king, right?"

"No problem," Kora said dismissively.

Champion of Seasons

The seven were on the gondola. Charon pushed it off the shore and it floated down the river. Throughout the trip, he kept the vessel steered in the right direction.

As the boat moved, Lyn's old pilgrims had some parting words for her.

"Live as a good and faithful person," said Father Triff. "Be pious, be faithful, be modest."

"Find a good man, marry him, and make passionate love to him," said Ella. "Life is too short to forgo love, romance, and the tender touch of a man."

"Lyn, have you been fighting?" asked Del. "If so, keep my blade, for you will get better use out of it than I would. Keep fighting and be strong!"

Champion of Seasons

"Have fun in life, Lyn," Jason said. "And don't always do as you're told—you do you! Only you know what you want!"

"Get married, have a family, and die a grandmother," said Paige. "Be surrounded by your loved ones as much as possible."

When the boat arrived at its destination, everyone disembarked and parted ways. The shades went in one direction. Lyn was about to go with them when Kora grabbed her arm. "This way, my escort," she whispered.

Eventually they found themselves at a set of iron gates that led to a stone pathway. As they approached, Lyn heard a snarl coming from near the gate. She placed her hand on her sword as they walked forward. That's when they saw it.

Champion of Seasons

The creature was about the size of a St. Bernard, with black fur and four huge paws. More terrifying was that it also had three dog heads attached to its body, all barking and growling as the two approached.

"Oh, dear God," Lyn uttered, about to pull her weapon. The massive thing was snapping at them.

Kora wasn't scared at all. Instead, she wore a gigantic smile as she shouted, "Cerbi!" As she approached the three-headed dog, the monstrosity calmed down. Kora proceeded to pet the animal, scratching him under his chins and along his sides and rubbing his belly. The three heads all looked like they were in dog heaven as Lyn sheathed her weapon at this bizarre spectacle.

Champion of Seasons

"Oh, who's a good boy? Who's a good boy?" Kora cooed to the beast as Lyn walked past and through the gate. Having gotten her fill of weird dog affection, Kora followed Lyn.

The two entered a field filled with white fuzzy wheat-sheaf-like flowers swaying in the wind. "This is the Asphodel Fields," Kora explained. "Named that, of course, because the field is mostly asphodel flowers."

"That's what these are?" Lyn commented as she took in the scenery until she saw something disturbing. Among the sheaves, swaying in the wind, she could swear she saw people, pure white like the flowers, mindlessly staring off as they swayed along with the asphodel.

Champion of Seasons

"Kora...I see people in there," Lyn remarked, sounding disturbed.

"Oh, yes." Kora turned to her. "The Asphodel Fields is where an unremarkable soul ends up—a normal person who's neither good nor evil. They become mindless shades in service of the Lord of the Underworld."

"Mindless!" Lyn jumped. "That sounds horrible!"

"Well, it's better than waiting a hundred years in Acheron, and it's far better than Tartarus, though not as good as lower-level Elysium. Of course, Elysium is a treat, not the default or the punishment."

"The afterlife in general sounds dreadful," Lyn said.

Champion of Seasons

"Yeah, you don't say," a grumpy voice called out from the fields.

Lyn and Kora turned to see the source of the voice—another shade in the field; only he was dressed in a toga. The rest of him was pure white, like the asphodel.

"Oh, hey, Tire!" Kora called out.

"Ha!" Tire tripped and fell on his face. He quickly got to his feet and looked up at Kora. This was when Lyn noticed his eyes were missing. "Your Highness, I didn't notice you were with this..." Tire rambled before noticing how alive Lyn was. "Wait, why travel with this squishy living being?"

"My guard was ambushed on the way back from Mother's house," Kora stated. "Lyn here is escorting me in his place. I must say she's doing a fine job!"

"*Again?*" Tire gawked. "'Cuz I could have sworn I heard Rhada saying you got attacked going from here to your mother's realm."

"And Lyn escorted me then as well, and she is quite competent!" Kora replied with a huge grin.

"Well, I think you should prepare yourself," Tire stated, "because your husband is aware of the ambush on your way to Elysium, and I'm sure he'd like to know what happened."

"Oh, how sweet of him to worry about me."

Tire sighed. "I hate the bastard for putting me in here, but I can't deny he loves you, Your Highness."

Champion of Seasons

"Thank you for the heads-up. I'll be careful," said Kora, smiling once more.

"You're why I still have my mind, Your Highness. I'd do anything for you!" Tire smiled back.

After Kora said goodbye, the two walked away. As they left earshot, Lyn asked, "Who was that?"

"Tire's the overseer of the field," Kora explained. "He's a gifted prophet, and I was able to have him keep his mind with some help from my husband."

"Your husband sounds powerful."

"That he is, and I'm learning from him. He taught me that trick with the undead I used when the yeti attacked us."

"Right," Lyn slowly said.

As the two continued their walk through the fields, eventually they reached a river. On the other side was a land that appeared to be on fire. Lyn saw lava and brimstone everywhere, so much that it glowed under the low light of the Underworld.

"That's Tartarus," Kora explained. "It's where the depraved and evil go to be punished for eternity. You see that volcano in the center of the island?" Lyn squinted through the smoke. "That's my father-in-law. Yeah, my husband had a rough childhood."

Suddenly a wayward tentacle came out of the water. A purple monster wrapped itself around Kora and began to pull. As Kora tried in vain to free herself, Lyn drew her weapon and swung it at the creature. The blade made purchase, but it wasn't enough to stop it the beast; it only

Champion of Seasons

slowed it down as more tentacles wrapped around Kora. Lyn got a good swipe at the thing, and Kora was able to get an arm out and knock on the ground in quick two-by-two rhythm. In the resulting chaos, the monster uncurled itself from Kora and slithered back into the river.

Lyn took a deep breath. Noticing Kora was looking at something behind her, she turned around. At first, all she saw was eyes. Red glowing eyes staring back at her, staring into her soul. The sensation was enough to have her trip over her own feet as she tried to back away. She then saw his skin. His pale, sickly skin. Next she took in his frail, wiry frame. Tall, he wore a black robe while he glared at her with piercing eyes.

Champion of Seasons

"Who are you and what is a living soul doing in my realm?" the man said, his voice echoing in a foreboding tenor. The look on his face was stern. Lyn held her sword in a wobbly hand while struggling to regain her footing.

"Ah!" Kora trilled in elation, breaking the tension in an anticlimactic fashion. "Darling!" She then ran up to the man with her arms open wide and nearly leapt into his arms. He took a step back to avoid falling as he held Kora in an embrace, his stern look giving way to a tender smile.

"This is Lyn. She's with me, hon," said Kora. "The guards my mother sent were ambushed, and she escorted me here."

Champion of Seasons

"Like my men were ambushed on your way to your mother's?" he asked. His question died in his throat as Kora kissed him over and over, making a darn-near disgusting display for Lyn as she stood up and sheathed her sword.

"Well, I guess I should be off then..." Lyn uttered before Kora said, "No, no, please stay the night. I think that's only fair, right, hon?"

"Where are my manners? Of course your escort can stay one night," her husband replied.

"Oh, thank you!" Kora squealed, and gave him a kiss.

She linked arms with him and gestured for Lyn to follow. Lyn shrugged and went along, hearing Kora enthusiastically ramble on about the journeys the two had taken, including the fights with the yeti, the kraken, and the bandits.

"I was able to perfect that trick you showed me!" Kora nodded to her beloved.

"Very good. I told you it would be of great use," he replied.

"Lyn is so skilled with the sword," Kora went on. "She's, like, a natural at it."

Lyn followed in silence, taking in the sight of the Asphodel Fields as they gave way to a stone building flanked by two menacing shades and the three-headed dog Kora had called "Cerbi." The building towered before them as an enormous line of ghosts, in double file, came from the shore where Charon had dropped them off to the entrance where they stood, waiting to be let in. Lyn followed Kora and her husband her to an entrance at the back of the building.

"This way," Kora whispered.

Lyn took in the very plain stone room, which led to a hallway. Kora's husband looked to his wife and to his guest. "This is where we will part, for now," he said. "I shall be in the manor later this evening, dear." His tone softened as he addressed Kora.

"Oh, yes, my welcoming dinner." Kora beamed as she turned to Lyn. "You're invited, of course!"

"Right," Lyn said as Kora's husband headed down the hallway and entered a room through a side door.

Kora gave her a smile. "He's going to judge souls. We're now in the House of Judgement."

Champion of Seasons

CHAPTER FIVE

A ruckus came from the room Kora's husband had entered. "You spent your lives marauding, pillaging, stealing, killing, and raping, and you have the absolute gall to demand mercy?"

"I was poor and had to feed my family," a familiar voice replied, muffled through the closed door.

"Is that...?" Kora muttered to Lyn.

Lyn nodded. "Yep...sounds like the leader of those bandits."

Champion of Seasons

"Poverty is no excuse for depravity!" Kora's husband angrily replied. "And raping that woman, slitting her throat after your boys razed her caravan, and slitting the throats of her young sons does not put food on your family's table or clothe them in any way!"

"You can't tell me you never have, you know, gotten lonely and needed your needs fulfilled," the bandit retorted.

"I've never had to do that by inflicting intentional pain on another person," Kora's husband thundered. "Your excuses wear on me."

"Me and my boys were killed by a cursed hag and a lady with a...*sword*!" the bandit replied. "Surely you must see we were defending ourselves from such a scourge. Imagine women with swords—how hellish is that?"

"I can judge them when they are here before me," Kora's husband replied. "Until then...didn't you draw your weapons before the aforementioned women and threaten to rape them? You can't say you defended yourself. You could have avoided what happened by leaving them be."

"So we're worse than an unlady-like lady and a witch?" the bandit asked angrily.

"You and your band are absolutely worse—I have a niece who wields swords quite skillfully, and being with magick is not a choice," Kora's husband retorted. "And the 'witch' you refer to is my wife! I will not hear any more. You are to go to

Champion of Seasons

Tartarus, where the Furies will have their way with your tender flesh!"

"I'm sorry. I'm sorry! Please...I didn't—" the bandit whimpered.

"You're only sorry you got caught and will be punished," Kora's husband bellowed. "Send the next person in."

"You see, he has a heart." Kora looked to Lyn with a wink. "He acts all stern and unemotional, but I can tell you he's moved by good music and the sight of wild nature."

"Right..." Lyn sighed.

Kora gestured for Lyn to follow. The two walked down the hallway and into a tunnel carved into obsidian, then headed up some stairs into a foyer. "This is the manor, and the dining room is this way!"

Champion of Seasons

The two walked into a stone room with red-and-blue carpeting and a dark wooden table with various foods on it. Much of it looked exotic to Lyn: mushroom biscuits, orange liquor, salad with pomegranate seeds and white leaves. Kora sat to the right of the head of the table; Lyn took a seat next to her by instinct. It didn't take long before others —red women with leathery wings, large men covered in chains, and ghosts—came to claim their seats.

There was also a pale woman clad entirely in black with black hair and eyes, followed by another more scholarly-looking woman with a torch lighting the way; the latter had almost glowing hair and wore silk robes. Kora gave her a wave.

Champion of Seasons

The scholarly-looking woman smiled and waved back. "It's good you made it. He was starting to fret. You know how he is," she stated while her associate nodded and sat down.

"Good thing I'm here, Hex!" Kora smiled back.

"Mm-hm," the black-clad woman said, disinterested.

"Oh, Hex works with my dearest," Kora told Lyn. "She's known him longer than I have."

"You don't worry that..." Lyn said. "I mean, she's pretty and all..."

"Oh, no. They're strictly on business terms. If he was going to do that, he would have by now and wouldn't need me."

"You have a lot of faith in him," Lyn remarked.

Champion of Seasons

"I trust him and know he trusts me." Kora grinned as a few regal-looking men came in to take their seats. One had gold jewelry all over him; Lyn recognised him as Rhada from Elysium.

Lyn stared in awe as Kora's husband, the foreboding-looking, red-eyed, pale-skinned gentleman in black robes, entered the room and stood by his seat at the head of the table. He then called out, "Everyone! Attention!" The room grew quiet. "A toast! To my lovely wife, Kora! Blessed be her return to this realm!" There was the clinking of glasses and a cheer and "Hear, hear!" as everyone dug in. Nervous, Lyn sat quietly as the rest of them discussed death, souls, the nature of fate, and mortality.

Champion of Seasons

"I heard you got Kora back here on your own," a woman in a white hooded robe with scales on her skin said to Lyn in a slow voice.

"Yeah," Lyn replied nervously.

"You are indeed someone of great virtue," the woman replied.

"Oh, Styx, you can't be serious," the pale woman with dark hair shot back. "She's a mere mortal."

"One who slayed a kraken and fought off bandits for Her Majesty," Styx retorted. "That indeed is a person of honour, and I can see where her vows lie."

"Can't be that hard to do," the other woman stated. "What is she in the grand scheme of things? How can this mere mortal do what our powerful servants could not?"

Champion of Seasons

"That is not to ponder but to accept, Nyx," Styx stated. "This mortal is no mere mortal."

"I would eventually be carrying her soul down all the same," a man in black robes with black feathered wings and a pale, bony face interjected. "Where she goes is not my concern—just getting her to Acheron is what I would need to do."

"If I know the king as well as I do..." Styx smiled. "...and I've known him a long time—I predict I will be involved in a parting ceremony, and, Than, your task and Charon's would be easy indeed."

"A...what?" Lyn muttered in shock.

"Do not worry yourself." Than smiled. "This will only come to pass upon your death, whenever that is."

Champion of Seasons

"You don't know when that is?" Lyn asked.

"None of us do." Styx nodded. "Not even the king knows that. That is a matter with the Fates."

"When the Fates go..." Nyx smiled cruelly before clapping her hands. The seismic sound this made grabbed everyone's attention.

"Nyx, your manners!" Hex chided.

When the dinner wound down, everyone headed off in their respective directions. Hex walked with Lyn. "I was told to show you to your room for the night, and that I will," she said. "You protected his beloved while taking her home, and I think she has made this place better...and made the king better."

Champion of Seasons

"You think so?" Lyn nervously replied, trying to make small talk.

"Oh, he was even more tight-lipped and miserable before. I think her charm has brought out the colour in him. I support their relationship."

Lyn looked puzzled. "It needs support?"

"Apparently." Hex sighed. "It's Kora's mother—she has never liked the king, and when those two wed, she swore to be his enemy. It's sad, really. He doesn't want to admit it, but when she isn't here, it really affects him."

When they reached Lyn's room, she entered and sat on the bed.

"Don't be afraid to explore the manor." Hex smiled. "And again, thank you!"

Champion of Seasons

With that, Lyn was alone in her room. She sat there for some time before she decided to get up and go for a walk. When she did, she passed the entrance to the library.

"So how is your mother doing?" Lyn overheard Kora's husband say in a soft tone.

"She's well, honey," Kora replied. "She's her usual obsessive self, but she's healthy and happy. She still asks if you've hurt me, though."

"Can't blame a mother for being worried about her children. Mine fought my own father to save my life and the lives of my brothers and sisters..." His voice trailed off.

Lyn peeked through the doorway to see Kora sitting on her husband's lap on a couch. Her beloved's eyes were staring right at Lyn, piercing her with his intent.

"Have you been eavesdropping?" he snapped.

"Sir, I am so sorry," Lyn replied quickly while taking a deep bow. "I was walking through the manor... Hex told me I had free reign for the night...and—"

"No one told you to listen in on people's conversations, though."

"I...I know..." Lyn got halfway up. "This is true, but I swear it wasn't my intent."

"Oh, come on, honey," Kora chimed in, her own piercing glare trained on her husband. "It wasn't like we said anything of controversy. Lyn has met my mother and she was in the hallway. You know what they say about hallways...something about them having ears or something."

A sigh came over him. "All right, because you have been so helpful, Lyn, all is forgiven. You may read in the library if you wish," he said with a faint smile.

Lyn walked in between the shelving units while Kora and her husband read a book together. Lyn looked over the tomes and the scrolls that lined the walls and shelves. After a time of thumbing through the books, she found a volume titled, *Maneuvers Into Battle: Be the Best of Balist Battle!* Lots of alliteration, but the cover had two men sparring on it. It reminded her of Rothan back in Mabe.

Lyn picked up the tome and began to read it. As the cover suggested, it contained diagrams and explanations of various battle tactics and fighting maneuvers, some of which she recognized from her training with Rothan, but with different names, and others she never had heard of but thought to ask Rothan about when she was back in Mabe.

She scanned the book for some time when "Whatcha readin'?" sounded from behind her shoulder. Lyn turned to see Kora give her a big smile. Lyn didn't have a chance to respond. "Oh! A book on battle tactics! Someone is into fighting! Is it that boy back in town?"

"I just...well, it might not be useful information." Lyn heaved a sigh as she went to put the book back on the shelf.

Kora stopped her with her arm. "Lyn, if it's what you're into, why hold yourself back?"

Champion of Seasons

"Well, it isn't something women are supposed to be into..." Lyn sighed again. "And it won't be something I'll need when I become a nun."

"Is that what you want?" Kora asked with a cocked head. "It doesn't sound like you're enthused about it."

"Well, it's what's expected of me. It's what Mother wants of me...and yet..." Lyn looked down to her shoes. "In this year...on these adventures, and with Rothan...I have never felt so alive. I just don't know."

"Yes, you do. You just said it—the life of a nun isn't what you want! I can tell you it isn't what the Fates want of you. Just because your mother wants it of you, or your community, doesn't mean that's what you were meant to do."

Champion of Seasons

Lyn stared at the book's cover then looked back at Kora. "My mother prepared me for this. I promised her I wouldn't need a man or be burdened with children."

"So? You promised that when you were too young to understand the world, right?" Lyn looked back to the floor. "I made a similar deal with my mother for the exact same reason," Kora continued. "The truth was that it wasn't the life I wanted. Now, Lyn, did that cute guard back in town change your mind? Or was it gripping a sword for the first time? When did you, in fact, realize your heart is that of a warrior? A guardian? A fighter?"

Lyn slumped to the floor, crying, hugging the book to her bosom. Kora sat next to her between the shelves of the library.

"Lyn..." Kora placed a hand on her friend's shoulder. "There's something I should confess: my guards were never killed either time. I sent them away—no one argues with a princess, or a queen, of a realm."

Lyn looked up at her. "What?" she asked with a look of horror. "Why do that?"

"I made up the story about the ambush to justify why I was there when I answered your prayer," Kora replied. Lyn looked up inquisitively. "You remember praying to the High God, asking to die on the mountain? I answered with *nope!*"

Champion of Seasons

"What! What are you?" Lyn blurted with a wide-eyed expression. "What exactly are you?"

Kora sat right up, and straightened her neck, and stared Lyn in the eyes with a powerful look, a look that pierced into Lyn's soul with a warm glow that wrapped itself all around.

Kora then said, "I am Persephone. Daughter of nature. Queen of the dead. I bring the spring and autumn. I bring life where life should not exist. I am evolution and adaptation. I am resilience and perseverance. I am delta. When you hate the path you are made to walk, or if the path you are walking crumbles to dust beneath your feet, I am your patron within the divine."

Champion of Seasons

Lyn stared back with a look of awe, dropping the book to the floor and bowing with one knee out. Kora stood up and bent down to place her hand on Lyn's chin. "Look at yourself," Kora continued. "You are so strong...stronger than you have ever known. Everything you have done—the fight with the kraken, and the bandits, and your help with the yeti—so much of that was you. You had all that within you. Such strength would be wasted if it had died on that mountain. Now rise! Your path is a warrior's path." Kora looked over Lyn's shoulder then back at Lyn. "Also, rise because the king of the dead is here," she quickly said.

Lyn almost leapt to her feet and looked behind her to see Kora's husband standing before them in all his regal might.

Champion of Seasons

"I knew it," he slowly said. "Rhada told me about the 'ambush' on your mother's men. He was in disbelief that such a thing could happen! I knew better—my guards were very capable, hon. And a second time around? Your mother wouldn't send incompetent fools either; I know her too well."

"No harm went to them, darling, and the fate line stated the coast was clear," Kora replied. "I wouldn't subject myself to unneeded risk."

"Oh, I know you wouldn't harm anyone on purpose; you have always had a big heart," Kora's husband went on. "I was concerned about the danger you put yourself in with the yeti, the kraken, those nasty bandits, and the tendril in Tartarus."

Champion of Seasons

"That pales to the dangers I could face from cosmic horrors," Kora replied. "Except for the tendril, it was all nothing a mortal with the strength of Lyn here couldn't handle."

There was a pause. "I should check up on Tiresias before bed," Kora uttered as she looked to Lyn. "You know where your room is."

Kora then took off. Lyn looked towards Kora's husband, then bent down to pick up the book. "I...I should...put this away..." Lyn stammered as she slid the book back onto the shelf.

"My beloved is right," he spoke in an even tone. "You are strong. I foresee the Fates making use out of you. Kora was right to answer your prayer. The world needs you. Not now but soon. Thank you for bringing my dear wife back home."

"Thank you, Your Majesty...and you're welcome," Lyn replied nervously.

Kora's husband let out a low chuckle. "Her mother has never approved of our union. She goes around telling everyone who'll listen that I kidnapped her! It's part of our deal—a deal that wouldn't have had to happen if my mother-in-law was willing to let go. Sooner or later, a mother will have to let go."

"Thank you for the wisdom." Lyn bowed her head. "If I may, I need to retire for the night and rest up for the journey home."

"Good night," he replied as he walked away.

Champion of Seasons

Lyn saw herself to her room and lay in the warm bed of satin and velvet. As she drifted to sleep, she thought on her adventures, trying to figure out where she fit within the grander scheme of things.

In the morning, she approached Charon on the boat, with Cerbi and Kora looking on. As she did, she saw the figure of Styx standing in the water by the shore, and the king of the underworld not that far off. "Let make this official," the king spoke as he gestured Lyn forward. She complied and walked towards the shore. "Kneel before me," the king sternly spoke. Lyn complied and went to one knee. Styx cupped some water into her hands and approached Lyn. Kora walked up to her husband's side.

Champion of Seasons

"As the queen of the dead and the daughter of nature, I hereby declare you, Lyn of Mabe, to be the Champion of Seasons!" Kora said in a soft yet powerful voice. Styx then splashed piercing-cold water onto Lyn's head. It was coldest water she had ever felt, possibly colder than ice somehow.

There was clapping from onlookers that rose into an ovation as the king commanded, "You may rise."

Lyn nervously nodded. "Thank you...for everything. I must be off now." She then boarded the boat to a waiting Charon, who picked up his oar.

Kora waved. "Best of luck and remember what I told you: walk the path you want!"

Champion of Seasons

Charon pushed the oar into the water and started across, and the boat sailed across the River Styx. After the short ride, Lyn disembarked and walked along the shore of Acheron, past forlorn ghosts vying for a spot on Charon's boat.

As she headed to the cave that led up to the surface, she pondered everything that had happened to her. How she had prayed to the High God, only for her prayer to be answered by one of the "lesser" gods of old. If this wasn't enough to talk her out of becoming a nun in service of the High God, then nothing would. Her faith in the High God had been broken, and there was no going back after her talk with Persephone.

When Lyn made it back to the surface, it was sunny but cold; winter had

Champion of Seasons

taken hold. Snow was on the ground and draped on the trees. Ice tinseled along the tree branches and shrubs along the path back to Mabe. By this time, it was nightfall, and the town was lit with fires to keep the homes warm.

Standing at the gate to the village was Rothan, sporting his armour. Frost beaded off his breastplate due to the trapped heat in his armour keeping him warm. When he spotted Lyn, he stood up from his slouched position. "Has it been taken care of?" he asked, trying but failing to hide his excitement. Lyn nodded. "So will you be joining the next pilgrimage?"

"Rothan, how do you feel about me?" Lyn asked.

"I...I missed you," he replied, staring at his greaves. "I missed our secret sparring sessions, and I just admire how strong and resilient you are. Having witnessed the violent deaths of your friends then having to fight those monsters..." He paused when Lyn bowed her head. "Lyn, you are...amazing!"

"Rothan, I've given this a lot of thought...and...did I tell you I prayed to the High God for death?" Rothan shook his head. "I survived, no thanks to him."

"Lyn, that is blasphemy...not that I would tell anyone," he automatically added.

"I can't be a nun of the High God—not after what I've been through and..." Lyn's voice trailed off before she grabbed the unsuspecting guard by the shoulders and planted a kiss on his lips. "I want to be with you," she stated in a weirdly

Champion of Seasons

enthusiastic tone as she gazed into Rothan's eyes. "I want you to know me every night you can! I want our lives to intertwine! Rothan, I can't do that as a nun!"

Rothan stood in shock. A blush came over his face as he stared back at Lyn. "Wow," he uttered dumbly. "I mean...I...I would love that too. But what about your mother?"

"Well, I know she wants the best for me," Lyn replied with a sorrowful look. "I'll deal with that fallout when the time comes. Eventually she'll get over it, I'm sure.

"Right..." Rothan stated with another blush. "Well, until then, welcome home and good night." As Lyn walked into the village, he called out, "Oh, Lyn. It

Champion of Seasons

isn't much, but I have a room in the village in case of emergencies. You can use it if things really go south between you and your mother. That way at least you won't be dependent on her."

Lyn smiled. "It will do. Thank you. I've held you up enough for the night. I should leave you to your post." Rothan nodded, and Lyn continued to walk.

Lyn's mother stopped talking to her when she announced she wasn't going on the next pilgrimage and had no interest in becoming a nun of the High God. "How could you?" she shouted at her. "That life is the best life you could possibly have!"

"So you think marrying Father and having me was a mistake?" Lyn shouted back, words she had uttered before but that now demanded an answer. "You would want no grandchildren? Have I really been such a burden on you and was Father really that bad?"

Perhaps her mother didn't really love either Lyn or Lyn's father. Perhaps her mother had wanted what she thought was an easy life and blamed her husband for being a farmer in a small village. Or it might have been the basic fact that Lyn was following a very different and oppositional spiritual path from her mother. This was something Lyn would never know the answer to and never truly understand.

What Lyn did know, five years later, was that she and Rothan were now mercenaries in the nearby community of Tides. Mostly they fought bandits and

Champion of Seasons

wild animals while protecting grain or escorting merchants—escorting being something Lyn was all too familiar with.

It had been five years since that strange pilgrimage and its aftermath. Years full of pain, adventure, and peculiar happenings.

Lyn awoke in the bed she shared with Rothan, to whom she had been married for three years now. It was a lean day, not like a feast day, which was the cycle of life for mercenaries. She was the first out of bed, with Rothan snoring soundly next to her, tuckered out from a night of passionate lovemaking. Lyn slipped on a robe and approached a shrine at the end of the room on the upper floor of their small homestead. The shrine was on a wooden box with an engraving of

Champion of Seasons

pomegranate seeds encased in the delta symbol. Lyn knelt on one knee and clasped her hands.

Moments later, Rothan woke up and got into a robe of his own. He rubbed the sand out of his eyes, approached Lyn from behind, and placed a hand on her shoulder. "'Morning," he said. "Still seeking favour from her?"

Lyn chuckled. "Well, she listens and answers…one way or another. I was forced on a path I didn't want. She showed me I could carve my own path in life, and it has been a good life so far."

"Well, why wait for her now?" Rothan asked. "You already escorted her —"

"Yes, that's me, the Pomegranate Escort, yeppie," Lyn replied with a shrill laugh.

"Don't knock it." Rothan sat next to her on the floor. "How many people can say a god has spoken to them?"

"Never mind that it's one of the old, 'lesser' gods," Lyn said. "Being with Kora made me realize this new god isn't the benevolent, all-powerful being we were all told he was."

"What are you going to do about it? Most people in our community are believers of the High God."

"For now, wait and let live what isn't in my way." Lyn grew serious as she looked back at the shrine. "Kora and her relations all told me the Fates had a plan for me. What that plan is...time will tell."

Manufactured by Amazon.ca
Acheson, AB